*A
Harlequin
Romance*

CASTLE OF THE UNICORN

by

GWEN WESTWOOD

HARLEQUIN BOOKS

Toronto • Canada   New York • New York

CASTLE OF THE UNICORN

First published in 1971 by Mills & Boon Limited,
17 - 19 Foley Street, London, England

Harlequin Canadian edition published October, 1971
Harlequin U.S. edition published January, 1972

CHAPTER ONE

As the plane lost height, the south-west of Africa un-
rolled itself like a map, thought Maggie. But if you
were trying to draw it, it would be rather dull because
there would be no use for bright colours, only rather
faded browns and yellows.

She forgot Matron's admonishment not to speak to
strange men during her journey and addressed her
neighbour.

'Is that the desert?'

The young man with the red hair and the rough-
hewn windburned features seemed to be a person of
few words, for all he replied to Maggie's question was
'Aye.' Then, glancing at the small figure beside him in
the drab beige suit with white high-necked blouse, at
the wide brown eyes and childlike expression beneath
the straight-cut fringe of hair that showed dark gold
under the schoolgirlish brown pudding basin of a hat,
he relaxed from his usual tongue-tied embarrassment
with women and added with a rolling of r's that betrayed his Scottish origin, 'Practically the whole
country is desert, but not your idea of desert, I dare
say. Plenty of dust and bush, but don't expect Christmas card stuff. No golden sands with camels and palm
trees here.'

'I didn't expect it,' said Maggie, although she had
been visualising something of the kind. But what
should she expect? She did not know.

She maintained a dignified silence for about two

minutes, but when she saw a darker, curving line of some kind of growth, could not resist asking, 'What are those squiggles?'

'Squiggles?' The young man frowned. 'Och, I see what you mean now. Those yonder are bushes along dry river-beds. A man can live here for ten years before he sees a river in flood. Would you credit it that river-beds where there are trees make fine places for picnics? You know what they say, if you fall into a river in Africa all you need to do is to dust yourself off.'

Maggie wondered whether she was supposed to laugh at this, but decided against it. The man's face still held a solemn expression, and in any case it was difficult to raise even a semblance of a smile when your stomach felt tied up in knots with excitement and, yes, with dread of the unknown. To distract her mind from this she decided to go on talking.

'Have you lived here long, Mr. . . .?'

'Angus MacRae. I've been here a wee while. I'm a geologist by profession and I like it fine here. Is this your first visit, Miss Young?'

It was not surprising that he knew her name. The label that Matron had tied on to her overnight bag was as big as one you would tie on to a child if you did not want it to get lost in a crowd.

'Yes, it is.' Then she added indiscreetly, or so Matron would have thought, 'But call me Maggie. I'm not used to being Miss Young.'

'Maggie? Was your mother or father Scots, then? For it's a good Scots name.'

'No, they were not Scots.'

Her brief reply seemed to quell Angus MacRae's somewhat limited attempts at being sociable and he lapsed into the silence which he had hitherto kept during the whole of the journey since he got on the plane in Johannesburg. If this was all that happened when you addressed remarks to strange men there seemed little harm in it, mused Maggie.

To take her mind off that tight knot in her stomach, she began to recapitulate in her mind the surprising events of the last two weeks. Perhaps she had sounded too reserved to the young man at her side when he asked her about her parents, but the truth was that she knew very little about them, for she had lived in a children's home since she was a small child. Because she had a happy disposition and could not remember any other kind of life, she had, for the most part, been perfectly contented with her environment. She was one of Matron's favourites, mainly because she gave so little trouble and helped with the other children, and this rather downright but kindly woman was all the mother she had ever known.

Sometimes, as she grew older and realised that there was a world beyond the Home, she imagined scenes in which some long-lost relative suddenly appeared at the door and whisked her away into a life of impossible glamour, but in her heart she knew that these dreams were on a par with the stories she made up for the younger children when she was helping Matron to put them to bed.

She had stayed on longer than usual at the Home because of this capacity for making herself useful, but she was now eighteen and was waiting for news of whether the authorities had approved of her ambition to do a course to fit her for welfare work. This had been Matron's idea since she felt that Maggie with her ability to get on with people would be well-fitted for this kind of career.

So when about two weeks ago she received a summons to Matron's office she had gone there with a hopeful heart thinking that there must be some news about her future plans. Indeed there was. But it was not the kind that Maggie had expected.

Maggie knew Matron so well, but today there was something a little odd about her expression as she regarded the girl through her sensible brown-framed spectacles.

'You remember, Maggie,' she said, 'I told you long ago when you were old enough to understand that you had been brought here when your mother and father were killed in a car crash.'

Maggie nodded.

'Although they had taken British nationality since the war and changed their name to an English one that was easier to pronounce, your father had been Polish and your mother French. Enquiries were made, of course, but it seemed there were no relatives left to take care of you. Both your parents had been active in the Resistance during the war and they came through it unhurt, only to lose their lives in this car crash some years later.'

Maggie had been about two years old when this happened and apparently she had been in the car as well but had escaped unharmed. Now it was like an old story that had no real connection with herself except that she felt a pang of sadness whenever she considered how ironic it was that her parents should have escaped such dangers and then, when their life together should have been peaceful, they had not lived very long to enjoy it.

'The neighbours said that they were overjoyed when you were born, because they were then quite old and had given up hope of having a child,' Matron had told her in a rare moment of expansiveness.

Maggie noticed now that Matron was holding a letter.

'I did not tell you before because I thought nothing might come of it, but a little while ago I had a visit from an attorney who had traced you to this Home. Some old friend of your parents had apparently just discovered your existence and wished to make some contact with you.'

Maggie felt her heart begin to beat fast.

'How very strange,' she said, 'after all these years!'

Matron nodded.

'Yes,' she replied a trifle ironically in her North Country accent. 'It's taken her a little while to find you, I must say.'

'Her?' asked Maggie. 'Who is it, then?'

Excitement suddenly mounted inside her and she felt that she could not wait another moment to hear all about it. How irritating Matron was with her slow ponderous way of getting to the point!

'But who is it? Oh, please, Matron, tell me quickly. If you don't, I feel I'll just burst!'

'Now don't get excited. Be sensible. It may not come to anything.'

'What might not? Oh, Matron, please tell.'

'She wants you to go to stay with her for a short holiday. It need not make any difference to your plans for the Welfare course, because that doesn't start any-way for another three months.'

'Oh, Matron, I'll die if you don't tell me all about it soon. Where does she live? I do hope it's by the sea. Do say it's Cornwall ... or even Brighton would do. In fact anywhere would be lovely.'

'No, it isn't Brighton,' said Matron, not even smiling. 'Now don't get so worked up, Maggie. I'm surprised at you—you're usually so sensible. It's South West Africa.'

'South West Africa? But where on earth is that?'

'It's where it says it is, of course.'

'But Africa ... how can I go there?'

Her first feeling was one of profound disappointment. Why had Matron told her all this when it was manifestly quite impossible? A holiday in Cornwall before she started her course would have been the most delightful thing that had ever happened to her ... but Africa! Her mind boggled at the fantastic nature of such a suggestion.

Matron, who had known Maggie a long time, read all these emotions in her young face.

'I don't know,' she said in her slow way, 'that it is so impossible. Although I'm not at all sure that it's a good idea to allow you to go out there to people you don't know. But she has offered to pay your fare. They must be fairly respectable folk, I should imagine, though after all that might not follow just because she's a Baroness and lives in a castle.'

'A Baroness ... a castle! Matron, are you teasing?'

But it was not Matron's habit to make light of things. The round kindly face was quite serious and the eyes grave behind the glinting spectacles.

'Sophia, Baroness von Linsingen, she signs herself, and the notepaper is headed "Castle of the Unicorn".'

'But it sounds like a fairytale! Oh, Matron, don't you think that someone might be joking with us?'

· Maggie wanted to believe, but could not bring herself to do so. The image that had arisen in her mind, a kind of Walt Disney palace with spires and turrets and pinnacles set upon a blue mountain, was childish, she knew. And the Baroness. She saw a good fairy god-mother kind of person, dignified but benevolent, beautiful as a dream, sitting high in a turret room, weaving spells that would bring her, Maggie, halfway across the world.

'It seems the place is run as a sheep farm,' announced Matron, shattering these dreams somewhat.

'A sheep farm?'

'You'd better read the letter. It might put you more in the picture.'

'It is with overwhelming happiness,' read Maggie, 'that I have heard of the success of our search for Marianne's child, the little Marguerite. Marianne was my beloved friend during those terrible years of war. Her outstanding gifts, her brilliance and beauty, are inextricably woven into the pattern of my past.

'Now my hopes are high that I will find her again in this precious child. Please, I beg of you, consent to send her just as soon as can be arranged. We live very simply now in our old German castle on the edge of the desert. Since my husband's death, I have lived in a rather re-tired manner, but Marguerite will not be dull, I assure you. My son, Stefan, is at home at this time, managing the sheep-farming part of our estate, and where he is life can never be boring, naughty one that he is! Too handsome for his own good, but very charming, I promise you, not only to his elderly mother.

'I do not travel any more, so I will have to save the joy of meeting Marguerite until she arrives at the *schloss*, but I will send my son to meet her at the airport and he will fly her to our home in his own plane.

'My heart is filled with delight when I think that in

11

a few days I may see Marianne's beloved child. It will be like seeing her dear self again, my lovely friend, with all the charm and fascination of her youth. What does she look like, I wonder, this little Marguerite? But no child of Marianne's could fail to be anything but highly cultured and exquisitely beautiful. I confess that at my age this should not matter, but, old as I am, I set much store by physical beauty.'

Maggie looked up from reading the letter and turned rather startled brown eyes to Matron as if she was seeking reassurance from the well-known homely face.

'It doesn't sound as if she's expecting anyone like me.'

Matron frowned and said flatly, 'And what's wrong with you, may I ask?'

'Well, it sounds as if she's expecting some kind of princess. Exquisitely beautiful, highly cultured.' Maggie gave a rueful laugh. 'It may sound like Marguerita Janovski, but it hardly fits Maggie Young, you must admit, Matron.'

'Oh, I don't know so much,' said Matron, trying to sound reassuring. 'You've had a good education up to your "A" levels. No one can say you didn't do well at school. And what's wrong with your looks? You have a good skin and nice eyes and your hair is a bit straight, but that's fashionable these days. It turns up quite nicely at the ends.'

Maggie sighed.

'She doesn't sound as if she'll be satisfied with that. She's obviously expecting some outstanding beauty. I wonder what my mother looked like? It should be interesting anyway. She'll be able to tell me. Maybe she'll even have photographs of my parents. I never had.'

'It's this young man I feel dubious about,' said Matron.

'What young man?'

'Stefan, her son, the one who's going to meet you. She sounds as if she dotes on him. Now, Maggie, I know you can be trusted. You've always been a sensible girl, but remember, be circumspect.'

Maggie laughed at Matron's old-fashioned turn of phrase.

'If he is her only son, I expect he's just horribly spoiled and she idolises him. He's probably quite ordinary really and not half as handsome as she thinks. Maybe she's the kind of person who thinks the ones she loves are very beautiful. She sees them through rose-coloured spectacles. In that case let's hope she's prepared to love me. She sounds rather a dear and terribly romantic,' Maggie added optimistically.

The next few weeks were busy ones for Maggie. The Baroness had paid for her return air ticket from London, but it did not seem to have occurred to her that Maggie might not have suitable clothes for a holiday in the heat and dryness of that part of Africa. Matron did her best with their small resources, but there was little money to spare and Maggie had to be content with various hand-me-downs that had been given to the Home by some benevolent society. She and Matron cut and stitched, trying to make them fit Maggie's slender figure, but they still did not look as if they had been intended for her in the first place.

The beige suit and white blouse in which she was

travelling had been of good quality when they were bought. Anyone could see that. But it did little to enhance her appearance.

'It's quiet and in good taste,' Matron assured her. 'You look very ladylike.'

'Yes,' replied Maggie, doubtfully.

It was rather loose on her and had the effect of making her small slim figure look painfully thin. Matron had dipped into her own pocket and bought Maggie two cotton dresses at a chain store, one a practical brown striped one, and the other a heavenly pink that suited the young girl's colouring and pleased her very much in spite of its cheap cut which she did not even notice. They were the first off-the-peg garments she had ever possessed and she thought they were perfectly beautiful.

'What can you wear in the evening?' worried Matron. 'People like that probably dress for dinner.'

'The pink dress,' said Maggie, surprised that there should be any doubt about it, but Matron disagreed.

Finally she found a black crêpe dress in the old clothes box and renovated it for Maggie with a lace fichu and an artificial rose.

'You can't go wrong with black for evening,' she assured Maggie when she showed her the results of her efforts, but Maggie did not feel she looked like herself at all in this creation. However, Matron was being so kind that she could not disappoint her by voicing her own doubts.

The poverty of her holiday clothes did not particularly worry her, for her life so far had been very far removed from any need for pretty, glamorous clothes. In the Home, your disposition mattered far more than your looks, and Maggie, with her gay practical nature, had been well suited to community life. In a way, with this background, she had been as secure as she would have been if she had had parents, for she was always surrounded by people who liked her and she had known only very fleeting sadness in her short life.

'We're getting near Windhoek now,' said her quiet neighbour. 'It's in a circle of mountains, so you land some way from the town.'

The desert scene had changed and Maggie could see high mountains in the distance. The sun was sinking far away beneath the rim of the distant desert, and colours of deep pastel were spreading over the sky from east to west.

'Well, here goes,' thought Maggie. 'Here's where you meet the Baroness's beloved son. You'd better make a good impression on him, my girl, for he seems very important to his dear mama.'

'Is someone meeting you, Miss Young?' asked Angus.

'I hope so. I'm going for a visit to . . .' She could not bring herself to say the romantic fairytale name to this stolid young man at her side. 'Someone who used to be a friend of my mother's, Baroness von Linsingen, has invited me to stay. She said her son would meet me.'

Why did Angus look so amazed?

'Stefan von Linsingen? He's coming to meet you?'

'Yes. Do you know him?'

'Everyone knows Stefan von Linsingen,' replied Angus. 'They could hardly help it.'

'Why do you say that? You sound as if you don't like him much.'

Angus laughed shortly.

'Stefan would never care a tinker's curse whether I liked him or not.'

'But what's wrong with him?'

'Nothing that you would notice.' Angus's blue eyes beneath the sandy brows were cold, or did she imagine that? 'He's the best karakul farmer in the district, the best rider, the best polo player, the best man in fact at any sport. He knows a hell of a lot about geology, archaeology, astronomy, in fact every subject that's useful in South West. Aye, he's brilliant and charming.'

'So why don't you like him?' Maggie asked.

'Because I've had one or two brushes with him and he is utterly ruthless with anyone who dares to oppose him. He's an out-and-out individualist. You either admire him tremendously or can't stand him.'

'Well, there's one thing,' said Maggie, smiling, 'he seems to have made you talk more than you've done during the whole journey, doesn't he?'

Angus laughed. Then something about her innocent brown gaze seemed to sober him.

'Take care,' he said. 'You may think I'm foolish to warn you when I hardly know you. And maybe you're a wee bit young for his taste, I'm thinking, but all the same, look out for him. He has a way with women, and not such a good way either. If you want to enjoy your holiday, I'd advise you to see as little of him as possible. He breaks hearts as easily as breaking eggs. It seems he has an irresistible charm where women are concerned, and it's not good for a young girl to get hurt that way.'

Maggie was astonished at his eloquence on the subject of Stefan von Linsingen. But he need not worry. Romance was the last thing she wanted at this stage in her life. She was more interested in studying to follow the profession she had chosen. But it would be interesting to meet this man. He did not sound the mother's

16

darling she had imagined from the letter of invitation.

However, when they disembarked at the crowded airport, there seemed to be no one there who fitted the Scotsman's description of Stefan. She stood rather forlornly with her one suitcase and presently Angus rejoined her as if he felt some responsibility for her in spite of their short acquaintance.

'He's no here yet,' he answered in reply to her question. 'He's a law to himself when it comes to time, but woe betide anyone who keeps him waiting.'

It was then that Maggie saw a tall figure hastening towards them. In spite of the fact that she had assured herself she was not interested in Stefan, her heart gave a lurch of disappointment. Why, he's old, she thought. But then the Baroness, Matron said, was much older than my mother. He's frightfully distinguished and handsome—but oh dear, I didn't think he would have grey hair. The man coming towards them looked as if he could be a film star, the kind who takes part in those gloriously romantic films about Venice or Rome, where the lonely girl on tour meets a handsome, suave, charming local inhabitant and falls in love with him to find at last that he is married already and only interested in an affair.

Maggie was surprised that Angus spoke very pleasantly to him considering his previous scathing remarks, But she supposed he had to be polite because of her.

'Herr von Linsingen, I'm glad to see you. This is the young lady who has come to visit the Baroness.'

His accent fitted his appearance.

'Marguerite? I am so sorry I am somewhat late.'

Rather to Maggie's embarrassment, he bowed over her hand and kissed it. Then keeping her hand in his he surveyed her with frank appraisal and a twinkling look, almost of amusement.

'Charming,' he said. 'A schoolgirl only. So young, so fresh. We have all been dying of curiosity to see you, my dear, but, forgive me, you do not look in the least like the portrait of your mother.'

'I've never seen one,' Maggie informed him.

'No? Well, no doubt that can be remedied. And Mr. MacRae?' He turned his charming smile upon Angus. 'How convenient for me that I should meet you like this. I was going to phone you while I was in Windhoek. I have a proposition to put to you about that expedition we discussed.'

'I'm glad you've come to meet Miss Young, Herr von Linsingen,' Angus said.

Maggie was surprised to see that the solemn Angus had relaxed and was even smiling. She felt puzzled. His obvious enmity towards Stefan when he had spoken of him previously seemed to have dissolved. How could he have spoken like that and now be behaving as if he liked him? Angus MacRae seemed such a straightforward person, yet although he had betrayed obvious dislike for Stefan von Linsingen here he was accepting his invitation to join them in their thirty-mile drive into the town, and becoming deeply involved in conversation with him. It sounded very technical, all about rocks. After he had given her that first gracious welcome as if he was putting a child at ease, Stefan had taken little further notice of Maggie.

Sitting in the back of the car, she felt as if she was indeed still a schoolgirl as she heard the two men talking about pigmatites and hydrothermal veins, whatever they might be. She looked out of the window of the large Mercedes that was bearing them effortlessly along the highway. As they rapidly approached the town, the sun had gone and the mountains all around were painted in purples, blues and greys, misted over with a shimmer of reddish gold.

She had understood that the castle was at some distance from Windhoek because the Baroness had written of Stefan flying them in his private plane. So where were they going now? Maggie felt rather forlorn and was sorry that Angus was taking up so much of Stefan's time. She would have liked to ask all kinds of things, but supposed she would get an opportunity later.

But how strange that this older-looking man with the look of suave worldly sophistication should be the forceful character that Angus had described! In her mind Maggie had visualised someone entirely different, someone younger and more rugged-looking, someone who looked reckless and devil-may-care.

I suppose people are never like you expect, she told herself. But what a hypocrite Angus is! Fancy giving me the impression that Stefan was difficult when this man seems so gentle and correct. Except that I do wish they would stop talking so scientifically and tell me something about the town.

As if reading her thoughts, Stefan turned to her, saying, 'Marguerite, forgive us. When we get on to the subject of gemstones, I'm afraid I forget all my manners. Look over there, my child. There is the famous Tintenpalast, that long building on a rise overlooking the town. When you see it during the day, you will admire the glorious gardens. Do you know that Tintenpalast means? But of course you are sure to speak German?'

'No, not at all.'

'Really? I suppose you have concentrated on French.

I have heard how accomplished your mother was at languages. Tintenpalast means the Palace of Ink. It is an affectionate name—how do you say, a nickname—for the Administration Building.'

Maggie had never had any opportunity to study languages and she felt a small rising of panic that the Baroness would expect her to be more accomplished than she was. Herr von Linsingen seemed to take it for granted that she would know these things.

Now Maggie noticed that most of the street names and notices were written in German and she commented on this, feeling at the same time awkwardly ignorant about her surroundings.

'South West was a colony of the German Empire for thirty years until 1915,' he informed her. He sounded so kind, thought Maggie, but like someone giving information to an ignorant child. Where was the impatient person that Angus had described?

'Windhoek is not a great city. In fact it is one of the smallest capital cities in the world. Its population amounts to only about forty thousand and it has no subways, no trams, no skyscrapers. But even now after all these years it has a little of the gay atmosphere of old Germany, especially at Carnival time when there are processions in the streets, a masked ball and all kinds of festivities.

'Oh yes, Marguerite, when you know this country you will find it a fascinating place. This charming, sophisticated city is only an hour's flight from primitive desert and the Skeleton coast where diamonds can be gathered from the shore.'

Maggie had not expected the imagined Stefan to be so eloquent. Although Angus had said he was clever, she had expected a man of deeds, not words, and certainly not this rather academic dissertation upon the country she was visiting.

Now they were driving down the main street, the Kaiserstrasse, Maggie noted that it was called. Even she could translate that, she thought. But imagine it still being called after a character in World War One!

'Alas,' said Stefan, 'many of the old German buildings have disappeared. All is now too modern for my taste.'

But the hotel was charming, still with the gables of a hostelry in Bavaria.

'You will join us for dinner, Angus?' Stefan insisted, rather to Maggie's surprise. Was she never to get a chance to ask questions? And what had happened to the Scotsman's animosity? He was smiling and nodding, saying, 'That would be a pleasure, Herr von Linsingen,' as if he had never spoken those bitter words about his host's character.

A smiling German maid showed her to her small pretty room with its white counterpane and wallpaper of cornflowers and poppies. In hesitant English she told Maggie she had not been here very long. Indeed she still had the rosy bloom of a northern country.

Maggie hastened to have a warm bath. Darkness had come as if someone had swiftly dropped an indigo curtain, and although it had been hot during the drive from the airport, now the temperature had become crisp and cool. There was a sort of sparkling exhilaration to the thin dry air as Maggie stood at her window watching the moon rise over the mountains beyond the town.

From somewhere among the cast-offs Matron had

produced a silk Japanese kimono decorated with cherry-blossom and butterflies with a background of azure blue. It looked a little quaint, but it was very pretty. Maggie stood on her balcony enjoying the feeling of well-being that the sparkling fresh air induced, her head flung back a little and her brown hair lifted softly by the night breeze.

Below her room there was a kind of courtyard, paved in stone with one or two strange potted plants, where people were sitting having drinks at white wrought-iron tables. She noticed one particular group which seemed very gay and she looked rather enviously at the girls with their beautifully tanned arms and legs and their shimmery dresses of light cool material. They looked so happy and confident. Her mind dwelt in some panic on the choice of the pink cotton dress or the heavy black crêpe to wear for dinner, and for the first time in her life she minded whether her clothes were suitable.

As she was watching the young girls who seemed so at home and sure of themselves with their male companions, good-looking young men in white long-trousered safari suits, they were joined by another man who came with long-legged stride across the courtyard to join their group.

Although he was immensely tall and broad, so that he seemed to dwarf the girls' normal-sized escorts, he walked with the easy grace of some wild animal, a leopard perhaps or a lion, for there was something leonine about the tawny gold of his hair as Maggie viewed it from her balcony. The others all seemed immensely pleased to see him and rather to Maggie's surprise he embraced each girl warmly with much laughter and chaffing from the rest of the company.

'He's a cool one,' she thought, as each girl melted into his arms to receive a passionate kiss, lingering there for as long as he chose they should remain.

'Don't often get to town these days ... must make up for lost time,' she heard him say in a deep baritone voice that seemed to have an unusually attractive accent to it.

'What are you doing here today?' she heard one of the girls ask. He had turned his back and she did not hear his reply, but he shrugged his shoulders and flung his arms wide, and they all burst into laughter as if he had said something very amusing.

She had been so interested in this scene that she had not bothered to conceal herself but was leaning over the little balcony without thought of being observed, but evidently one of the group noticed the little figure in its picturesque gown and in a few seconds, much to her embarrassment, they were all looking up at her. The lion man, as she thought of him, came walking across until he was directly below.

Putting his hand with exaggerated drama upon his heart, he called, 'Juliet, or is it Madam Butterfly? Come down, come down from your balcony and let us buy you a drink. My friends here have need of an extra girl this evening.'

Maggie shook her head. She was considerably embarrassed by the attention she and the young man were receiving from the rest of the people in the courtyard. All eyes seemed to be concentrated upon her and she wished to goodness she had remained in her room.

'Don't refuse us, Madam Butterfly,' the young man called up. 'I can vouch for the respectability of my friends, if not for my own. Won't you join us?'

Maggie found the courage to speak.

'No, no, thank you, I'm afraid I can't.'

Her voice sounded horribly self-conscious and stilted.

The other members of the party were laughing and someone shouted out, 'Let this be a lesson to you, man, for trying to pick up fascinating little Geisha girls. For once in your life you're not proving irresistible!'

'We'll see about that,' Maggie's tormentor replied, and he seized a guitar from the band that was performing in the courtyard and proceeded to sing 'O Sole Mio' to her in a deep baritone.

She turned away and sought her room. It seemed the only way to get rid of him. But even there she could still hear his voice, this time a stupid falsetto singing the aria 'One Fine Day' from *Madam Butterfly* and then his normal deep voice rang out in an imitation of a Victorian male singing 'Come into the garden, Maud'. Would he never stop? She thought of going out again to try to quell him as she had sometimes quelled unruly boys at the Home, but could not imagine that the sternest voice she could muster would have much effect on this man.

However, finally he gave up and she heard the laughing crowd departing, still singing as they left. Her hands trembled as she changed into the pink dress. What an obnoxious creature! How could he make her so conspicuous? She hoped sincerely she need never see him again. Well, that was hardly likely since she was to leave Windhoek tomorrow.

Maggie had never stayed in a hotel before, and as a consequence of the serenading episode she felt self-conscious and quite sure that everyone was staring and laughing at her. It was good to see Angus and Stefan waiting for her in the lounge. Whatever Angus had said about Stefan no one could criticise his manners now. He handed her into a chair with the utmost thought for her comfort and complimented her on her dress. This was kind of him, she thought, for she could see that it was not really grand enough when compared with the other women's. They all looked astonishingly chic and Continental as if they were in Europe, not Africa.

'What would you like to drink, Marguerite? Lemon? Orange? Lime? Or something stronger?'

Stefan still had that rather amused twinkle when he regarded her as if he was still surprised by her youthful appearance. She chose an orange drink while Angus had a beer and Stefan drank whisky. She was glad that he did not consult her about the meal, for she was completely bewildered by the menu she had been handed. Why, it's almost as long as a book, she thought. I would never know what to choose. But Stefan, who had evidently noticed her confusion, gently guided her to his own choice of what he thought suitable. He's so nice, she thought, he would never embarrass anyone like that horrible brash lion man, for she was still smarting at the thought that people might giggle and whisper when she entered the dining-room.

'There will be four of us at table,' she heard Stefan tell the waiter. 'Herr von Linsingen will doubtless agree with my order. I know his tastes. If not, he can alter it to suit himself.'

The waiter smilingly withdrew.

Maggie looked up, startled.

'Is there another member of the family here that I'm to meet?'

'Yes, my dear, I should have told you. I'm afraid Angus and I were so busy talking that I omitted to offer his apologies. My nephew Stefan was to have met you, but he found himself involved with some urgent business of his own. So I offered to meet you instead and drive you to the hotel. However, you will meet Stefan at dinner, I hope.'

'Stefan?' Maggie stammered. 'But then ... I don't understand ... who are you?'

The grey-haired man looked utterly astounded.

'My dear, forgive me. I did not for a moment realise you thought ... I am Boris von Linsingen, Stefan's uncle, but here comes Stefan now.'

'Sorry, Boris,' said the young man, confronting them. 'I'm a spot late. Urgent business. Couldn't avoid it. You know how it is.'

He sounded very breezy, thought Maggie, not in the least sorry.

'Yes, Stefan,' replied Boris gravely. 'I know how it always is when you hit town. However, I am hoping you will give us the pleasure of your company at dinner at least. This is Marguerite, your mother's guest.'

Stefan looked at her closely. She felt he took in every detail of her appearance. Then his laugh rang out so that all the other guests in the lounge looked over to their table and smiled.

'Madam Butterfly in person! So I'm to have dinner in your company after all?'

For Stefan was the lion man, towering over her chair.

'I'm quite sure our mothers' old friendship makes us kissing cousins,' he said, grinning.

And before she could protest, he lifted her up so that her feet swung from the floor as if he was picking up a child and gave her a firm warm kiss. Then he held her by the shoulders and gazed at her quizzically while she felt the warm blushes rising over her cheeks.

'Why, Boris, she's just a teeny-weeny little girl, not even grown up yet. Maman is going to be very, very surprised!'

CHAPTER TWO

MAGGIE had never dined in a large hotel before and the array of implements at her place startled her a little. Boris must have noticed her dismayed glance, for he signalled to the major-domo to have removed all but those that were really necessary.

'We are only having three courses. There is no need to clutter the table with all this silver,' he said.

Maggie was impressed by this high-handed dealing with the man who with his immaculate appearance looked like a lord himself. She settled down to enjoy the first course, which was really delicious.

'Do you like this, my dear?' asked Boris, noting her appreciation.

'Of course she likes it,' said Stefan. 'Who would not?'

'It's heavenly,' Maggie agreed. 'What is it?'

Stefan burst into delighted laughter.

'It's smoked salmon and caviare, my love. Don't say you don't recognise it. In my experience every girl knows the most expensive things to order. Surely you're no exception.'

Maggie was nettled.

'I'm not your love and I've never tasted it before,' she replied flatly. 'Where I come from, they don't have caviare. In fact it's a treat to be given fish and chips.'

Stefan was not in the least put out by Maggie's ill humour. He stroked her arm gently.

'Sorry, luv,' he said, pronouncing it in an imitation of her accent. 'Can't supply the chips tonight. But isn't it nice to be dining with a capitalist like Boris here for a change?'

Angus frowned at Stefan and said, 'I can swear people have better manners where Maggie comes from even though they don't eat caviare.'

By their looks Maggie was afraid Angus and Stefan were going to have another of those differences she had heard about on the plane, but Boris hastily summoned the waiter to serve the wine.

'Champagne for our guest,' he said after he had tasted it, and taking the bottle himself he poured some into the tulip-shaped glass in front of her. Maggie, who had never before drunk anything stronger than lemonade, now had great difficulty in showing her appreciation of this wine that tasted to her unsophisticated palate very like fizzy vinegar. She took one or two mouthfuls, then set it aside and addressed herself to the next course.

'I ordered baby chicken for you, Marguerite, because that is very English dish, no?' said Boris.

Maggie regarded the small bird in front of her with some misgiving. It looked very bony and small. Where should she start? She had put a tentative fork into the bird's meagre breast when the waiter arrived back again at the table and with a flourish put in front of her a small bowl upon the top of which floated a couple of green nasturtium leaves. Here was a new problem. What was this? It must be the sauce for the chicken, because there was no gravy on her plate, perhaps some kind of wine sauce, for it looked very thin and colourless. She had heard that you could eat nasturtium leaves, though she had never tried.

Well, here goes, she thought and seizing a spoon in front of her proceeded to ladle the sauce on to her plate.

'Here, Maggie, hold on!' cried Stefan, exploding into what she thought was very irritating laughter. She paused, spoon in hand in mid-air, and looking around saw them all regarding her with startled eyes, while even the waiter seemed to be preserving his blank expression with some difficulty.

'That's for washing, not tasting, Marguerite, my love,' said Stefan. She blushed in confusion and hastily put down the spoon. At the same time she saw someone at the next table dipping her fingers into a bowl and delicately drying them on a napkin. Oh, why couldn't she have seen this before?

It was difficult to keep back tears of chagrin as she struggled to cut the flesh off the horrid little creature that seemed determined to bounce all over her plate. As if he was trying to console her Boris ordered a very elaborate ice-cream confection for the third course, but by that time her appetite had gone and she spooned her way through this sickly dish until in the end she began to feel quite unwell.

She became more and more quiet, for although she was usually fairly poised and self-confident with people, the strangeness of her surroundings and the unaccustomed manners of her companions made everything she said sound foolish in her own ears.

'Would you like to go to the courtyard to join in the dancing?' asked Boris kindly when they had finished dinner.

She was just about to refuse when Stefan said, 'Sorry, Boris, I'm afraid I can't oblige. I have another engagement after dinner.'

He left them, thought Maggie, with not very well concealed relief. How she wished she had been able to get in her refusal first! Now she said to the others that she was tired after the journey and must get in some sleep if she was to be ready for an early start, for it was obvious to her that Angus and Boris were eager to get down to some technical talk.

But in spite of her excuse she lay awake a long time thinking of all the new impressions she had gained in the short space of a day since she had left London Airport. She could not help feeling some doubt about whether she would fit into this new environment with ease. 'Well, Maggie,' she seemed to hear Matron's north-country voice, 'you can only do you best. You can't do more.' Anyhow it's not for long, she thought. The Baroness had loved her mother, so surely she would love her, and on that hopeful thought she fell asleep.

The airport from which private planes took off was much nearer to the town than the one for commercial aviation. Boris had asked Angus to drive them out there in the Mercedes and then to return it to the garage where apparently it was kept for the sole purpose of providing transport for the von Linsingen family when any of them came into town. Last night Stefan had brushed aside Boris's suggestion that they should drive out together next morning, saying that he would need to get there earlier in order to prepare the plane. But when they reached there he had not yet arrived.

The older man's suave manner was ruffled. '*Gott in Himmel*,' he muttered, 'how inconsiderate is this nephew of mine! We will have to kick our heels here for at least half an hour after he has come, for he will have to see to the plane. It is he who should have arrived first, not us.'

But now a sleek sports car could be seen approaching at a very fast rate and stopped within view of Boris and Maggie. 'There he is!' exclaimed Boris, and started to move towards the car, but then checked himself and returned to Maggie. It was obvious why he did this, for Stefan and the other occupant of the front seat were wrapped in a passionate embrace, oblivious of all onlookers. Maggie caught a glimpse of silver-blonde hair and a turquoise sleeveless dress, then Stefan vaulted over the low door and, with a wave of her hand, the owner of the sports car drove away, hair streaming in the wind.

'Who was that?' Maggie could not help asking Boris.

Boris shrugged his shoulders and flung out his hands with a very Continental gesture.

'It is Carola. I did not know she was back. Sophia will not be pleased when she hears of this.'

When they eventually began the flight it was very different from that of yesterday in the smooth jet that had covered the miles with the effortless precision of an airborne train. Now the desert was with them all the time, not something far away, just to be seen on landing. Across the dry scrub the sun was rising, red, distorted by the morning haze. Below only the bush that looked black from the air broke the desolation of the greyish yellow ground. Waves of heat clashing with the cold updraughts made the plane buck like an untamed horse.

It was a four-seater plane and Maggie had been allocated the seat next to Stefan. When the plane dropped in a down-draught like a falling leaf it did not seem to perturb him one bit. He grinned and adjusted the controls with the utmost nonchalance as if, thought Maggie rather indignantly, he was riding a spirited horse.

But why should his skill make her feel cross? It was just as well for them all that he seemed to be able to manage the plane in these difficult desert conditions. She could hear him singing above the noise of the engine. 'O Sole Mio!' he carolled, shooting a glance at her that was full of mischief. What an infuriating creature he was with his blithe self-confidence and his conviction that the world was his to command. He just assumed all the time that with his charm he would be welcome anywhere. Whereas she herself ... again she began to worry about what the Baroness might think of her.

The trembly feeling in her inside she put down at first to nerves, and tried to ignore it. She had never travelled in a small plane before, especially in these rough conditions, and the excitement of yesterday's journey, the rich food to which she was unaccustomed, the heat and her conflicting emotions all worked together now and produced a feeling of nausea which she tried in vain to quell.

Boris, sitting behind her, would keep tapping her shoulder, making her twist round while he pointed out something on the ground below. The only way she could keep well, she felt, was to sit with eyes fixed dead ahead into space, but she could hardly ignore Boris's attempts to interest her in the countryside. Each time she would glance quickly at the reeling ground and then nod and resume her strained upright position.

'What can I do?' she thought desperately. 'I can't be sick in front of them. I can hardly ask him to stop, though I wish I could. In fact I feel so awful it would be a great pleasure to jump out of this wretched plane.'

At that moment she felt a large bag thrust into her hands.

'Just in case you need it,' shouted Stefan cheerfully. 'You're looking a spot green.'

The next few moments were a nightmare of shame for Maggie, but, when the bag was finally disposed of, she found she was feeling much better. Boris, all contrition for not noticing her state of health, produced some cologne from his overnight bag. He looked just the kind of man who would use it, thought Maggie: But she accepted it gratefully and in a while was a little more revived. Nevertheless she was very relieved when Stefan pointed below and shouted, 'Here we are. Won't be long now.'

At first she could see only the same desolate countryside, parched bush, sand and stones. Nothing moved in the vast expanse. But there over to the right as the plane dipped its wings she saw something green, and could it be ... the glint of water? This time when Boris pointed below she was all eagerness to view the scene.

The *schloss* or castle was difficult to see, merging as it did with the reddish brown colour of the landscape. From the air it seemed to crouch below on its little hill. Gone were Maggie's ideas of towering pinnacles and turrets. It was more like a child's model of a soldier's fortress, square and strong with battlemented walls and four corner towers set around a quadrangle.

They landed on a small airfield beyond the castle and when Stefan had taxied the plane into the hangar, Maggie noticed there was a jeep-type vehicle waiting for them and in this Stefan drove the little way to the gates. These were heavy double doors like those in some medieval fortress, bound in brass and studded with great metal bosses upon stout oak. Maggie wondered where on earth the wood had come from in this landscape whose only trees seemed to be the straggling

34

peppercorns at the gate.

The doors swung open and it seemed that Maggie's dreams of a magic castle were being fulfilled, for the gatekeeper was the quaintest figure she had ever seen, a little brown man like Rumpelstiltskin, about four and a half feet tall, with elfin face, brown and wizened, and pointed ears like those of some small wild animal.

'Hi, Samgau,' Stefan saluted him. 'Why were you not at the air-slip to meet the plane?'

'Very sorry, sir, the Madam keep me long, long, with all the things that must be done for this young miss.'

He looked with kindly curiosity at Maggie, his hand to his brow, his eyes screwed and wrinkled against the sun as they must have been for countless years.

'This is Samgau,' said Stefan. 'He's a tame Bushman, who was found half dead as a child wandering in the desert and has lived here ever since.'

'Why, he doesn't look any bigger than a child now,' Maggie commented when he was out of hearing.

'Bushmen are a strange living phenomenon,' explained Boris in his rather academic way. 'They are a kind of caveman survival, the most primitive people living. They live deep in the desert where no one else could survive, only themselves with their fantastic knowledge of desert conditions.'

Maggie felt a fleeting curiosity in what Boris was telling her, but it was eclipsed by her wonder at the scene in front of her eyes. She gasped in astonishment, 'Why, how beautiful! I never expected...'

It was in truth like coming upon an oasis in the middle of the desert. The castle was built around a quadrangle and in this was a beautiful garden with green lawns, strange exotic shrubs and, the most wonderful thing of all, a cascading fountain in the middle bursting out from the natural rock formation.

'Before the castle was built here, it was known as the Place of the Three Springs. That, of course, is why my father built in this particular spot, for one must be sure of one's water supply and springs are rarer than gold, certainly rarer than diamonds in this dry country,' Stefan explained.

The beautiful front doors were of moulded bronze, like the pictures of doors of old churches that Maggie had seen in books about Europe. But instead of religious emblems, the door seemed alive with bronze mouldings of animals, elephants with enormous ears outstretched, lions guarding their prey and antelopes tossing their proud heads.

She had very little time to inspect it, however, before it was opened by a most imposing figure. Immensely tall, the African woman welcoming them with grave dignity was made even more so by the high headdress that was of brilliant scarlet and similar to a turban. But her style of dress was the most surprising thing about her, for she wore a costume that seemed to date back more than a hundred years in time. It was of nineteenth-century style with a high bodice, and leg-of-mutton sleeves, and the brilliant folds of the voluminous skirt swept the ground as she moved away from Maggie directing her into the hallway of the castle.

'This is Serafina,' Boris informed her. 'She is Sophia's housekeeper.'

Serafina bowed gravely in acknowledgement of Maggie's greeting, and spoke some words in a strange tongue, but almost immediately after this she spoke in English, perfect even if spoken with a slight accent in a voice that sounded like liquid gold.

'She is a Herero woman,' Boris whispered as she

swept away as if propelled by wheels. 'That is their usual dress, not a fancy costume. The fashion is based on the dresses worn by German missionaries' wives who worked amongst their tribe a hundred years ago.'

'She looks beautiful, so stately and dignified,' Maggie replied. 'It must be wonderful to be as tall as that,' she added wistfully.

Stefan, who was listening to this, laughed heartily, while Maggie reflected that she inevitably seemed to amuse him whenever she opened her mouth.

'You sound like a small rabbit wanting to be a giraffe. I'm sure you could find an African folk tale to match your wish. But take care. In the folk tales there's always a moral that you should be content to remain as you are.'

The beautiful front door opened in to a rectangular hallway, which seemed as in some castle in the Middle Ages to be the heart of the house. The stone-flagging on the floor threw up an atmosphere of coolness so that, for a moment, coming in from the outside heat, Maggie had the impression that it must be air-conditioned.

Two exquisite crystal chandeliers made of hundreds of intricately fashioned pieces of glass hung from the high ceiling. The floor was strewn with Persian rugs which depicted hunting scenes, while panelled walls were hung with pictures of horses and with pistols, daggers and swords, their hilts magnificently worked with chased gold, silver and precious stones.

There was a heavy carved table so long that it seemed to take up a vast amount of the hall's centre and this was surrounded by highbacked chairs upholstered in green antique velvet. A sweeping stairway rose up to a musicians' gallery which filled the upper part of the hall at the back.

As Maggie looked up, the figure of a woman appeared and slowly descended to the lower hall. The Baroness—for who else could it be?—looked almost as much a part of the Middle Ages as her home. Maggie had imagined a fairy godmother, but no, this was the Snow Queen, she thought, somehow miraculously translated from her arctic home to the wilds of Africa.

Her pale grey gown matched her hair with its silvery gleam. Diamonds sparkled frostily at her throat amongst the cobwebby white lace and glittered from her ears beneath the swept-back smooth waves of her perfect coiffure. In front of her, making swift eager progress whereas she was slow, came two of the most beautiful dogs Maggie had ever seen, white wolfhounds of incredible slenderness and grace. They rushed to Stefan, putting their paws on his shoulders as he fondled them. Then, 'Down, Sasha. Down, Giselle,' he said as he went forward to help his mother down the remaining stairs. Her rather stern face softened as she embraced him and leaning on his arm she hastened towards them, but before she reached them Boris had taken Maggie's hand and was leading her towards the old lady.

'Sophia, my dear,' he said, the voice with its attractive accent coming gently and could it be warningly as he gripped Maggie's hand in his? 'Here is the little Marguerite for whom you have waited so long.'

The piercing grey eyes above the aquiline nose stared fixedly into Maggie's brown ones. Sophia's expression did not change. Only her voice, that of an old lady, wavered a little. Was the emotion it betrayed that of joy or was it surprise? Her hands were astonishingly strong as she took Maggie by the shoulders and turned her face towards the light that was streaming from the open door behind them.

'Marguerite! Welcome, my dear. I have looked forward so long to your coming.'

The beautiful patrician face so close to her own held an enigmatic expression as if good manners dictated the withholding of some strong emotion.

How should she address the Baroness? Maggie wondered in some bewilderment.

'It is very kind of you to ask me to visit you,' she ventured timidly, her slightly north-country accent sounding very pronounced to her own ears amidst all these foreign-sounding ones.

'How English she sounds!' exclaimed the Baroness. 'How odd that my dear Marianne's child should be so dissimilar. But there, when we have got to know you better we will probably find you have much in common with your dear mother—isn't that so, my child?'

'I don't know,' replied Maggie, feeling she had been found wanting. Why did everybody she met reduce her to a state of tongue-tied simplicity, she wondered, when usually she was quite happy to meet strangers? But they were not strangers like these. She bent her head and caressed the long silky nose of the female wolfhound—Giselle, was it? Well, here at least was one living thing that was friendly. The animal pressed up against her, lifting intelligent brown eyes to look into her face.

'And so now you have met my wicked Stefan, what do you think of him?' asked Sophia, glancing at her tall son with open adoration.

'What a question, Maman!' exclaimed Stefan. 'How can this poor child answer that to your satisfaction? She hardly knows me, but already I venture to say that Miss Maggie disapproves of me.'

'And no wonder,' said Sophia, tapping his arm sharply with the beautiful lace fan that she carried and taking another look at Maggie. 'What have you been doing to her, Stefan? She looks like a kitten that has been caught in a hedge. Serafina will show you to your room and we will all meet in a little while for an aperitif before lunch. Ask for anything you may need, my child.'

The room to which the tall Herero woman directed her was on the second floor in one of the corner turrets so that its walls were rounded on the outside and the curving window formed a deep embrasure, a window-seat looking out over the plain that stretched to the foothills of distant mountains. It was like a parkland although consisting of dry barren country with sandy wastes covered with little bushes growing in scanty brown tufts.

Inside the room the walls were of stone with a fireplace that formed a deep alcove. The furnishing was simple but very old, a bed with an intricately carved headboard, a wardrobe with panelling in checkerboard inlay. A small bathroom had been contrived from what had apparently been a clothes closet and this was luxuriously fitted with taps and towel-holders in the shape of silver dolphins. More Persian rugs in jewel-like colours were scattered on the stone-flagged floor and the bedspread was in an ornate design of red and blue.

Maggie was still wearing the beige suit. She unpacked a clean blouse and, discarding the jacket, washed her face, ventured to use a little rose-coloured lipstick and combed her straight brown hair. Today it was not even turning up at the ends. She gazed at her reflection in the mirror of the checkerboard wardrobe feeling thoroughly dissatisfied with herself. Did she really look as pale as that, or was it just the old mirror? One thing was certain, she had never looked plainer. A lost kitten, indeed! The Baroness had been very polite, but it had been obvious, thought Maggie, that she was not quite up to the standard that the old lady had been expecting.

As for Stefan ... well, she had never met anyone she found more annoying. She hoped he would be kept busy with his sheep for most of her holiday. Looking out of the window over the vast stretches of open land, for the first time in her life she felt acutely depressed. Already she was missing the friendly bustle of the Children's Home. She could not imagine what there would be to keep her occupied in this strange place. And Matron had said the Baroness was expecting her to stay for a whole month!

When she descended the stairs, she found that the hall was empty except for the two dogs, Sasha and Giselle, who were lying for coolness upon the flagged floor. However, she could hear voices coming from the room to the right of the staircase, so rather timidly she went towards the open door.

It was a large drawing-room like a European salon, furnished and decorated in white and gold. The faded golds of the Aubusson carpet with its wreaths of pastel flowers harmonised exquisitely with the dainty brocade chairs and sofas of French origin with their gilded frames. A beautiful intricately moulded white and gold fireplace was half hidden by an embroidered tapestry firescreen of incredibly fine embroidery.

Pausing hesitantly on the threshold of this lovely room, she heard the voices of the Baroness and her son, slightly raised as if they were having some discussion upon which they did not altogether agree.

'Confess it, Maman, you were astonished when you saw her.'

'I must agree, Stefan, my dear, she was not as I had imagined. Nevertheless, it does not alter the fact that she is Marianne's child and as such eminently suitable as far as I am concerned.'

Stefan laughed in a charming, persuasive way.

'Darling Maman, so obstinate when you've evolved a little plan of your own! The whole idea is absurd. She's just a child. I can't agree to your scheme. I never have. And now you've seen her you must admit I have every reason to doubt its success.'

Maggie heard the Baroness sigh. 'I wish you would be more amenable, Stefan. There is so much at stake.'

Were they talking about her? Maggie wondered. They must be. But then what was this plan they spoke of? She wavered on the threshold, wondering how on earth she could enter without appearing to have overheard this conversation.

'She is young, yes,' she heard the Baroness say musingly, 'but that makes her more malleable, more easily influenced. First impressions are not always the right ones, my Stefan. The way she dresses is a disaster, but that can be easily remedied. Nevertheless I do confess to having been a little disappointed. I expected a little more poise from Marianne's child.'

At that moment Giselle who had awakened and seen Maggie hovering at the door bounded into the room ahead of her and made it easy for her to follow. Sophia's expression changed quickly to one of a hostess's smiling welcome and Stefan asked Maggie what she would like to drink.

When she asked for a lemonade he said, 'Nonsense.

You've been ill and you still look pale. I'm going to give you a weak brandy and soda.'

When she protested, he proclaimed, 'Purely medicinal—Doctor Stefan's orders,' and thrust it into her hand. She had never tasted brandy before and after the first sip thought she did not want to taste it again, but she sipped doggedly at the queer-tasting liquid and in a little while was surprised to feel that it was doing her good. The queasiness which had made her nervous to face lunch had departed and she began to experience a sensation of relaxation and well-being very different from her previous tense emotion.

Lunch, served not in the central hall but in a small comfortable room on the opposite side to the drawing-room, consisted of delicious fish salad, veal cutlets and smoked breast of goose served with dark rye bread. Boris had produced a slim green bottle of Riesling wine to drink to their meeting, he explained to Maggie.

The wine, served in beautifully shaped clear-glass goblets, was pale gold in colour, deliciously cold and smooth to the palate. Maggie was thirsty and she did not realise how often the attentive Boris refilled her glass. Although the wine was light, Maggie had had no experience of drinking anything with an alcoholic content and the brandy had already done its work. From being abnormally quiet, she suddenly found that she seemed to be monopolising the conversation. Encouraged wickedly by Stefan, who was amused by her transformation from a prim silent little miss into one who was talkatively vivacious, she told them stories about the Home and gave opinions on all kinds of subjects which she had not previously known she possessed.

'So you intend to be a career girl?' asked Stefan,

when she had confided her ambitions to do a social degree.

'Certainly,' nodded Maggie, and was surprised to find it a little difficult to get her tongue round the word.

'But what about marriage?' asked Stefan with a wicked grin.

'Marriage? I've never even thought of it.'

'Oh, come now,' Stefan protested. 'In my experience every young girl thinks of marriage.'

'In your exsh ... experience, maybe. But let me tell you, Stefan, I wouldn't consider marriage even if ...'

She had been going to say even if the Prince of Wales asked her, but she could not remember what she had intended to say.

'Even if someone as charming as me asked you?' grinned Stefan.

'Never,' said Maggie. 'Even if you were the last man in the world, Stefan, I could never marry you.'

'*In vino veritas*,' said Stefan, and glanced at his mother. She was sitting stiffly and had not contributed anything to the conversation for some time. Now she rose and motioned the others towards the drawing-room. But pausing by Maggie, she pressed her arm and said in a voice like tinkling icicles, 'Marguerite, my dear, I suggest you go to lie down. The journey has tired you more than you realise. I will send Serafina with coffee to your room. Rest until five then you can come to my room for tea. We must have a little talk.'

All Maggie's vivacity drained away as she saw the disapproving face of her hostess and, followed closely by Giselle, she mounted the stairs to her room.

CHAPTER THREE

When Maggie awoke in her tower room after a refreshing sleep, she felt more her usual self. Perhaps it was true that on a jet flight you left part of your soul behind. Certainly she had felt disorientated and confused ever since she arrived here. It was ridiculous and unlike her to feel so subdued and meek with these strangers. But when at last she had become talkative because of the wine, the Baroness had looked very disapproving.

However, Maggie resolved now that she felt recovered from the journey she would try to meet with her hostess's approval. She brushed her hair until it shone, put on her pink dress with lipstick to match and rang for Serafina to direct her to the private sitting-room of the Baroness.

This was a small, more homely room than the big drawing-room, furnished in an English fashion with rosy chintzes and tables and small bureau of polished rosewood. There were photographs too which Maggie longed to inspect, but she sat sedately on a small armless chair while Serafina brought the silver kettle on its spirit lamp and the fine china teaset, the plates of small sandwiches and petits fours.

It was very different from tea at the Home where they had sat at table with Maggie at the head wielding a large enamel teapot while the children drank from serviceable cups and munched thick bread and butter and jam. At weekends there was slab fruit cake as a treat. Now she felt nervous as she balanced the paper-thin cup above its saucer and nibbled at a very minute sandwich.

Once more she seemed to have said the wrong thing to Sophia, for when handing the silver plate to her the Baroness had said, 'I don't know whether you care for paté de foie gras?' and Maggie, eager to please, had replied, 'Oh yes, thank you. I can eat anything.' What had she said to make the Baroness smile and quickly glance away? It was all very puzzling. Was there something special about ... what had she called it? ... paté de foie ... it tasted like some nice kind of meat paste to Maggie.

Her heart sank as Sophia began to cross-examine her. Obviously she wanted to know about her upbringing and, although up to now Maggie had thought her education very adequate, to Sophia it was apparently sadly lacking in the finer things of life.

'Music, my dear. I hope you have made a thorough study of the great masters. I think a grounding in the classics in early youth is essential.'

'I belonged to a choir,' Maggie stammered. 'We sang choruses from *The Messiah* last Christmas as well as carols.'

'That is good, but not exactly what I had in mind. I hope you were taken regularly to concerts.'

'Oh yes, we had concerts,' Maggie responded eagerly. 'It was great fun. One year we acted Cinderella and I was the prince, and another time ...'

Her voice tailed off as she saw the Baroness's patently pained expression.

'Doubtless home theatricals can be very amusing, but I was referring to the great artists of the age.'

What did she mean? thought Maggie, bewildered

again. Artists? I thought we were talking about music.

'Pianists, singers, violinists,' added Sophia. 'I hope you are acquainted with their performances by hearing their records at least.'

Maggie thought of the Home, the Saturday night hops where they danced with each other as partners and played old pop records. What chance had she ever had to hear good music?

'And languages?' The Baroness was continuing the catechism. 'You are acquainted, I take it, with French and German. Every child studies that at school, of course. But how are your Italian and Spanish?'

'I don't know French or German,' Maggie confessed, anxious to get this matter straight. 'I didn't do languages at school. Matron thought it would be best if I did domestic science subjects. I'm good at needlework. I could help with your mending ... or in the kitchen perhaps, though I only know plain cooking.'

'Our staff are very well trained and there is no need for our guests to help in the kitchen. As for needlework, the Herero women are masters at mending. They learn it at the mission schools. Forgive me, my dear,' said Sophia, for something in Maggie's expression must have conveyed her embarrassment. 'I did not mean to offend you. I was only eager to learn what education the daughter of my dear friend possessed. I feel I owe it to her memory now that I have found you to make up in some way for my long years of neglect.'

'But there's no need for you to worry about me at all,' declared Maggie. 'I've been happy all my life. Perhaps the life at the Home wasn't so wonderful. I don't suppose you would think it was, but it suited me, and now I've left school I know what I want to do. I'll be quite content to do social work, or if they don't think I can do that I could be a domestic science teacher or take a job as a help at a Home too. It's very good of you to have me here for a holiday, but you need feel no responsibility for me.'

Having made this long speech, Maggie felt better. She felt at last that she had asserted herself and thrown off all the insidious influences of this place that made her feel somehow inferior.

Sophia rose and moved to take something from the bureau drawer, then she came to Maggie and put it into her hands. It was an exquisite miniature. From the oval frame a beautiful face gazed out at Maggie.

'This is my mother?' asked Maggie, all her offended feelings of the last few minutes pacified.

'Your mother and my very dear friend,' the Baroness assented.

Poised, lovely, serene, she was every child's dream mother. No wonder Sophia was disappointed when she first saw me, thought Maggie.

'No one could know her without loving her,' Sophia said. 'She was, as you can see, very beautiful, but she also had a brilliant brain. She had travelled widely with her grandparents, for her own parents, like yours, had died when she was very young. The life she led with them made her very knowledgeable, good at languages, with a vast knowledge of music, opera and the concert halls of Europe, but with all this she was emotional and passionate. That is why she took so easily to life in the Resistance movement. Who would have thought,' she said musingly as if to herself, 'that this young lady who had led such an elegant life could have faced all the dangers she was called upon to endure? But that was later. When I first met her she was the most attractive, adorable creature I had ever met, always dressed like a princess.'

'This was before the war?' asked Maggie.

'Naturally. It was only after the war that I married for a second time and came out to this country. Stefan, as you will have realised, is the beloved, longed-for son of my old age.

'Perhaps you can realise, Marguerite, how pleased I am I have found you. Now perhaps I can repay in part the affection your mother always gave me. I have been thinking how I can do this and I have a plan in mind ... but more of that later. At the moment I have a proposition to put to you. I think it would be a good idea if you stayed here for about six months and learned foreign languages.'

'Here?' asked Maggie, thoroughly disconcerted by this idea. This must have been what they were discussing and perhaps Stefan did not want her to stay for such a long time. 'But who would...?'

'Boris could be your teacher. He is extremely good at conveying any kind of knowledge, and needless to say I would help with conversation.'

'But why?' asked Maggie, gathering up her courage to oppose the Baroness. 'I admit it's a good idea to learn languages, but it's not essential to the career I have chosen and I can't waste time. I must get on with my training.'

'Let me be frank, my dear,' said Sophia. 'The career you have chosen does not seem suitable for Marianne's daughter. I had thought when you have acquired a little more knowledge of French and some other tuition in, shall we say, life's little elegances, my dear Marguerite, we would send you to travel in Europe and perhaps to visit some of my relatives there. Now don't look so alarmed. It would not be for very long.

49

And by that time you would be more suitable...' She broke off rather abruptly.

'For what?' demanded Maggie. 'All this is very good of you and I know you're doing what you think is best, but I'm very contented to go on as I am.'

'We will see,' Sophia nodded enigmatically. 'Perhaps I have hurried you too much, my dear child, but I am so eager to do this for the sake of your dear mother, and for my own sake too. And Stefan.'

'But what has Stefan to do with this?'

Sophia looked slightly confused.

'Nothing. Nothing at all. But now I will ring for him and he can have the pleasure of showing you around the castle. When you have seen how comfortable and happy we are here and how many diverse interests there are perhaps you will not be so eager to leave us.'

Sophia had managed to make Maggie feel in the wrong, but how could she contemplate the idea of staying here for six months and then travelling in Europe? Obviously the Baroness was living in the past. People like me don't need that kind of education, thought Maggie. How I wish I'd never come now! It's all getting too complicated.

But she felt even worse when Stefan was summoned to show her around the castle. In reply to his mother's question he said that he had just come in from riding to inspect some sheep, and it was obvious that he was not very pleased to be given the task of showing Maggie around.

'Boris has the history of the castle much more at his fingertips, Maman. He enjoys showing it to people.'

'But I would like you to show Marguerite the castle,' his mother said firmly. A look passed between them, c letermined on her side, ironic on his.

'Very well, Maman,' he acquiesced. 'Of course it will be a pleasure. I had only thought that Boris is better informed.'

Stefan was dressed just as he had come in from riding, but even in the tight khaki whipcord jodhpurs and butcher blue open-necked shirt, Maggie had to admit that he had a striking appearance. It was owing to his great height, she decided, and the proud set of his head with its tawny mop of hair and clearcut hawk-like features. His eyes were of such a dark stormy grey that on some occasions they seemed almost black. Maybe that was a sign of displeasure, thought Maggie when she noticed this.

'There is really no need to show me around the castle,' she protested. 'I can easily wait until Boris has time...'

'Good grief, am I such a dangerous character that you're afraid to come with me? I assure you that I won't lock you up in a secret cell or anything like that. Besides, you should have realised by now that Maman's word is law. She's not used to being crossed. When she's decided upon a plan of action she usually gets her own way.'

Not with me, thought Maggie, but Stefan looks as if he could be like that too. So what happens when they both decide on opposing plans of action? What was that they used to say at school about when an irresistible force meets an immovable object?

'The *schloss* was built by my nostalgic grandfather,' Stefan was saying. 'It isn't as old as it looks, of course, just an imitation of the Middle Ages. However, the art treasures and furniture are genuine enough.'

They had paused by two chairs exquisitely carved

with golden crowns atop the high backs and the carved figure of a woman against each leg like the figurehead of a ship.

'These belonged to some ruler of Austria.'

Two enormous carved wardrobes bore the dates, 1710 and 1715, and on all sides were pictures of horses and hunting scenes and portraits of fierce Prussian-looking soldiers with high helmets and impressive moustaches.

'My father was Austrian, of course. My mother married the enemy. That is why they came back to live here after the war. Her family in Poland considered it a disgrace that Maman should have married him. She has never returned to Europe.'

So the Snow Queen had remained here on the edge of the wild desert, thought Maggie. What a strange destiny for one who had been used to the life of the aristocracy in Europe! They had reached a turret high above the green oasis and beyond stretched the barren plain with the ranges of dark hills in the distance.

'And away over there is the desert,' Stefan said. 'Grey dust turning to great white sand-dunes as it nears the coast. They're the highest dunes in the world and they lie on the edge of the cold grey Atlantic. There's no more inhospitable place. It's called Skeleton coast for it has been responsible for more wrecks than anyone knows. And yet it's there they find diamonds.'

'And why was this castle given its name?' asked Maggie, who had been longing to know this ever since she came.

'Oh, that's easy,' laughed Stefan. His grey eyes lightened and he favoured her with a brilliant smile. 'Nothing to do with fairytales, really. The oryx used to be plentiful around here in the early days. It's a particular kind of antelope that people think was the origin of the unicorn story. When it stands sideways it looks as if it only has one horn.'

He put out his hand and touched her cheek.

'If you keep on looking at me in that way with those large brown eyes, I'll have to think of more fairytales to please you. Only a maiden pure in heart can catch a unicorn with a chain of pure gold. We will have to see if it works with an oryx.'

He put his arm around her to steady her down the steep stone steps from the tower and she was surprised by a sensation entirely new in her experience. After all, she decided, it was true that Stefan could be very attractive. Perhaps her first judgement had been too hasty. But then she remembered Angus's warning. She must guard against his flirtatious manners, for she had seen him with other girls and she knew that with him charming women was just a way of life.

When they went outside into the beautiful garden, Maggie was enchanted by the romantic setting of the castle. Here there had been created a haven of coolness. Low walls were decorated in Delft tiles of blue and white design, and white doves flew from their stone cote to rest in the dark green leaves of tropical shrubs. Blue water-lilies floated on the pool near the fountain and now and again one caught the bronze metallic shimmer of a lurking fish.

'It is known as the Garden of Love,' Stefan explained, 'because my grandfather created it for his young bride who was very homesick for the green country she had left behind.'

'No wonder,' said Maggie, 'but how did they get all the building materials here to build the castle itself?'

'What a practical little soul you are! Here I am trying to be romantic and you talk about building supplies! It was quite a task. The stone was cut here in the mountains, but all the rest had to be brought by ox-wagon. My grandfather used to supply the workmen with an enormous supply of beer so that they would be content to work here. You can imagine what a thirst they had while labouring here in the heat of the sun.'

He shrugged his shoulders.

'It probably seems an absurd, antiquated kind of life to you, Maggie, come straight from London, but there's something about this life here that I would find hard to give up. I travelled all over the world when I was very young. Perhaps I was rather wild then. Certainly my father thought so. But I always returned here. This is my home.' An enigmatic, sad look had somehow replaced that attractive smile. 'Have you had enough of sightseeing now? It will soon be time to dress for dinner.'

'Yes, of course,' Maggie responded meekly, although she was enjoying this tour of the castle and would have liked to spend longer in finding out about its inhabitants. But Stefan, who had been unwilling in the first place to show her around, had obviously had enough. Maggie, who had previously vowed that she would avoid Stefan's company for the duration of her stay, now felt strangely snubbed.

So that when during dinner Boris was particularly attentive to her she was grateful and responsive to him. Tonight she had worn the black dress, but it looked even less right to her now than it had when Matron had altered it. The Baroness gave it one swift glance and averted her eyes. Stefan noticed that she looked somehow wrong, but he was absorbed in some thoughts of his own and paid very little attention to Maggie.

It was Boris with his naturally kind dispostion who was touched by her waiflike appearance. He thought she looked like a child dressed up in her mother's clothes.

'Have you any plans for this evening, or may I take Marguerite to see my workshop?' he asked Sophia, when they had drunk coffee from fragile Meissen cups patterned in blue and gold.

'Certainly,' said Sophia, 'if she will be interested.'

'What kind of workshop?' asked Maggie.

'He polishes semi-precious stones that he collects from his expeditions into the desert,' explained Stefan. 'Ah, I see Marguerite's eyes are alight with expectation. Show me a woman who doesn't sparkle with greed at the idea of seeing precious gems and longs to possess them.'

Maggie thought this was hardly just, since she had never in her life possessed any jewellery nor even thought about it. She was, however, intrigued at the idea of the suave Boris exploring the desert. There seemed to be so many facets to the characters of the people she had met since she came here.

Boris took her to a room in the castle that she had not previously visited. As he touched a switch the room was flooded with light and she could see several strong oak tables dispersed about the room on which were reflector floodlight types of gooseneck lamps above various machines of a kind Maggie had never seen before. There were different wheels for sawing, for grinding and for polishing, but before Boris attempted to demonstrate the machinery he first showed her some of the rough stone and next stone of the finished results of his work.

'I didn't know you could get stone in such glorious colours,' exclaimed Maggie. 'Whatever is it?'

'This is nothing very valuable,' Boris told her. 'Just various kinds of quartz. There is a tremendous variety of colour in the rocks of South West Africa. Rose quartz is the most common of the desert stones. But of course you get other kinds ... variegated quartz, bronze and orange in colour, blue lace quartz, and some smoky and some in a clear lemon colour.

'All kinds of more precious stones are found too. Heliodore, greenish yellow opalescent stones, and aquamarines that are more difficult to cut than diamonds, bottle-green tourmalines and a kind of turquoise speckled in blue and gold, gold topaz, agates in smoky grey and pink, blue chalcedony, orangy-green jasper. They are all more fascinating than diamonds.'

Boris demonstrated how the rocks were first cut with diamond saw blades, next ground with abrasive wheels and then sanded and polished with a solid felt wheel until a brilliant and fantastically smooth surface was produced.

He showed her some of the smooth beautiful stones set in silver and gold in the form of bracelets and pendants and there were plaques depicting African birds formed from the glowing coloured polished gems.

'How do you like this little chap?' he asked, placing in her hand a small pink elephant made of rose quartz, glossily polished and beautifully carved.

'He's enchanting,' smiled Maggie.

'Keep it,' he said as she was going to hand it back. 'Aren't elephants supposed to bring good fortune?'

As he led her to a leather armchair and proceeded to brew coffee in an electric percolator, Maggie reflected that she needed some good fortune to enable her to cope with all the new experiences that were coming her way. She felt a little forlorn and homesick in spite of Boris's company, and something of her thoughts must have been reflected in her expression, for Boris said, as he handed her the coffee, 'You look sad, Marguerite. Is anything worrying you?'

She had received nothing but kindness from him since she came here, so it seemed ungrateful to complain, but looking at his concerned expression on the face that was so like that of a distinguished middle-aged film star, she exclaimed, 'It's just that it's all so difficult. Sophia expects me to stay here and be educated. Then she proposes to send me to Europe to relations for a while. She didn't seem to want to listen when I told her I was perfectly happy with my own life and my own plans for the future. I hate to be ungrateful, but I only came here expecting a short holiday. I never expected to stay longer.'

Boris looked a little confused.

'She did not explain what her plans were for you before you came here, then?'

'No. At least not that I know of. Matron told me she had asked me here for a holiday. I thought it would only be a matter of weeks. I had no idea she would want me to stay.' She recalled what Boris had said and looked at him suspiciously. 'What plans are you talking about, Boris? Do you know why she wants me to do all this?'

Boris looked embarrassed.

'Yes, I do, but I would prefer that she told you herself, or otherwise . . .'

He did not finish what he had been going to say, but instead got up from his chair and started showing her a beautiful collection of polished stones of all descriptions that had been left in the barrel to tumble and had acquired a most beautiful finish.

'Choose some and I will make you a bracelet,' he promised. Maggie thought he seemed to be trying to divert her attention by offering her a distraction. It was how one would treat a child. But I'm grown up, she thought rebelliously, and I can chose whether I stay here or not. I don't have to do what the Baroness says.

CHAPTER FOUR

'HAVE you ever ridden a camel, Maggie?' asked Stefan.

He knew that she was usually called Maggie and had now adopted this way of address, rather to his mother's disapproval.

Maggie looked startled.

'I've never even met one,' she declared. 'In fact, Angus, the young man I met on the plane, was very adamant about telling me that I mustn't expect palm trees and camels in this kind of desert.'

'Ah, but he didn't reckon with the fact that one can import them if necessary,' Stefan asserted. 'I brought them from Arabia and they are very beautiful and very highly bred. They belonged to the stable of an Oriental potentate. I had great difficulty persuading him to let me buy them.'

'But why did you want them?' asked Maggie.

'Because when I see anything beautiful, whether it be a horse or a camel or merely a woman, I feel a desire to possess it,' declared Stefan.

'Then it's a good thing I was born clever instead of beautiful,' said Maggie, remembering one of Matron's sayings.

'Darling Maggie, you always have an answer, don't you?'

In the few days that Maggie had been here she had lost a little of her first awe of her surroundings and become more familiar with the people in the castle, especially Stefan. In spite of the fact that he thought rather highly of himself, she could not help enjoying his company. He was fun to be with and his attitude towards her seemed to have changed from indifference to something that was friendly and gay. He still treated her like an amusing child, teasing her without mercy, but he seemed to do that with everyone, even his dignified mother.

That morning he had decided to take her riding around the estate on one of the camels of which he was so proud. She wore her white shirt and an old pair of cotton jeans that Matron had packed 'just in case'.

The stables were beautifully built of the same stone as the castle.

'They are so luxurious,' Maggie told Stefan. 'One almost expects to see you have provided Persian rugs inside.'

'Wait until you see the dog kennels,' Stefan told her. 'Each one is built of stone and has a crest above the door as well as small turrets around the roof.'

Samgau, the little Bushman, had led the camels into the paved yard.

'Here they are,' said Stefan proudly. 'Let me introduce you to Kagara and Chaunu.'

'Where did they get such strange names?' asked Maggie.

'Tell her, Samgau,' Stefan instructed the little groom.

'Kagara is the thunder, Chaunu the lightning. Chaunu married Kagara's sister, but he treated her unkindly and Kagara came to fetch her away from him. They had a big fight in the sky, but were turned into clouds. So when there is a storm they fight again and their blood makes rain.'

'Rather a gory way to get rain, isn't it?' asked Stefan.

'No wonder we don't get much here.'

'You had better ride Kagara, as he's a little better-tempered than Chaunu. Don't you agree that they're beautiful?'

Maggie regarded them doubtfully. They were white and beautifully groomed and most handsome, but they had that superior look of contempt for the world that only a camel can achieve. She felt she would never dare to persuade the proud Kagara to carry her.

At a word of command, however, Kagara knelt upon the ground and Maggie had no choice but to accept Stefan's advice and sit sideways upon the fine red saddle that was tooled in a pattern of gold. She clung with more determination than dignity to this as Kagara rose with ponderous motion, flinging her backwards and forwards on her precarious perch.

At first Samgau led her 'just until you get used to it', Stefan said. Maggie felt in the first few minutes that she never would be able to get used to riding a camel if she tried for a thousand years. As they picked their way amongst the stunted bushes and rough ground outside the castle, the motion was like that of a ship at sea.

Fortunately she was so busy concentrating on keeping on the animal and trying to come down at the same pace as its trot that she did not have time to feel sick. As she bounced around on the saddle she looked at Stefan who was riding in front to guide her on the best path. In cream cord jodhpurs and brilliantly white shirt and wearing a sun helmet, he looked as much at home riding a camel as he had seemed when piloting his plane. The sun helmet he had insisted that she wear was too big and kept slipping over her eyes.

She felt the same waves of annoyance with Stefan as she had felt on the plane. Why was he so accomplished at everything? It made him seem so superior to ordinary human beings. But she was distracted from these thoughts by the discovery that all around them in this dry-looking country covered only by small scrubby bush and shining silvery grass, there were small black sheep.

She wondered how on earth they could get enough to keep them alive in this wilderness. She must ask Stefan, but at the moment conversation was difficult. All she could strive to do was to cling to her camel. Samgau had given up guiding her and was trotting at her side with an easy loping pace. He had been going like this for a couple of miles now, yet did not appear to be out of breath.

Apparently out of nowhere there suddenly appeared a shed with a windmill and a dam near by and Stefan headed his camel towards this spot. He was soon in earnest conversation with a farm manager and had apparently forgotten all about the fact that Maggie did not know how to get down from the camel. At last with Samgua's help she was able to descend and look about her. Stefan seemed to ignore her existence after he had effected a very hasty introduction to the sunburnt man who had emerged from the shed.

She sat in the shade on a box and looked at the landscape over which they had come. There was so much of it, so much vast emptiness with the blue sky stretching endlessly to the far horizon and only an occasional red kestrel hawk soaring in the heights. The flattish country was bordered by small hills covered by black bushes where here and there the hot breeze was whipping up dust devils. This morning had been cool, but now nearer midday the air seemed to tremble in the heat.

Mr. Edwards, the manager, produced a cool drink for her from a small fridge while he and Stefan drank beer.

'What kind of sheep are those black ones?' she asked.

Mr. Edwards looked at her as if he half suspected she was joking with him. Then meeting the enquiring gaze of Maggie's large brown eyes, he said mildly, 'Those are Karakul sheep, Miss Young.'

'But what are they kept for? I thought black sheep were no good for making woollen garments?'

The manager looked helplessly at Stefan.

'Good grief, Maggie, don't you know anything about karakul or Persian lamb?'

'No. Should I?'

'Well, it's quite evident you don't take much interest in fashion. Paris designers fall over themselves to buy our pelts and make them up into all kinds of luxurious garments. We call it Swakara now to distinguish it from the Russian and Afghanistan varieties.'

'But how do you cut the fleece from off the sheep? It looks so flat, not as woolly as the ordinary kind?'

Mr. Edwards flushed brick red and moved away ostensibly to speak to one of the labourers, but Stefan answered her with patience like a person who humours a child asking awkward questions.

'Ah, that's the twenty-thousand-dollar question, isn't it, Edwards? Unfortunately there's no way to take off the lamb's pelt without disposing of the lamb.'

'You mean you kill them?' asked Maggie, wide-eyed.

'Well,' said Stefan, 'Mr. Edwards here doesn't like to use that word, and the word "slaughter" is completely forbidden. We say a lamb is "taken" or "pelted". It's all very humane, however, and the lambs are only one day old when they are taken, so don't have much sensibility at that age.'

'Only one day old? But what about the sheep that lose their lambs?'

'Show me a sheep that's a good mother and then I'll feel sorry for her. No, Maggie, sheep are pretty dumb on the whole. You needn't feel over sorry for them. Wait until I show you some of the magnificent results of the karakul industry. The skins made up into a coat look like black watered silk.'

'All the same,' said Maggie, 'I don't think I'd like to wear one.'

Stefan gave an impatient sigh.

'You really are an exasperating child! Do you mean to say you would refuse one if it was given to you?'

'Yes.'

'You'd better join me on one of my trips to Paris. I go there once a year to study fashion in karakul. It's not so much to study fur as change of fashion. One year it may be short coats that are the rage, then heavier pelts will do. Next year the fashion is for maxi coats, then lighter pelts are needed. We used to throw away spotted pelts, but now they're fashionable with the young.'

'Well, it doesn't seem right to me killing day-old lambs,' asserted Maggie, stubbornly keeping to the original subject.

Stefan gave a cross exclamation.

'You eat meat, don't you? What's the difference?'

'I don't know, but it seems different.'

'What feminine logic! Just wait until you can see some of the fur fashions. I'll show you one of the Italian books when I get back. No woman could resist them.'

'Well, I guess I will never have the chance to own a

Swakara coat,' said Maggie, 'so I won't let it worry me.'

'If you married a karakul farmer you would have to wear one in winter as a matter of prestige.'

'Well, that's not likely to happen either,' Maggie answered in a matter-of-fact way. 'I'm more likely to be wearing a nurse's cape next winter.'

'Don't be too sure.'

Something in the way Stefan said this surprised Maggie. He was gazing quizzically at her from his superior height, but there was something in his expression that made her feel somehow scared. How stupid she was, she thought, to feel that she could be made to fall in with Sophia's plans for her future against her will, for that was what Stefan must be referring to. And yet there was something else, as if Stefan had a secret that amused him.

Did he think it was a joke that Sophia wanted to try to educate her? Perhaps he thought it was a waste of time trying to make her highly cultured. If so she would just show him ... but no, she did not intend to fall in with Sophia's plans at all. In a few weeks' time she would be back in London where at least she would not have to ride camels.

That afternoon, Sophia sent Serafina to summon her to a tea session. As she changed into the brown-and-white-striped cotton dress her heart sank at the idea of another hour of Sophia's persuasive methods, for in spite of her opposition to the Baroness's ideas she was falling more and more under the spell of her charm.

But it seemed the Baroness had given up discussing Maggie's future. She had another idea in mind.

'Marguerite, my dear,' she said, as she poured China tea into the delicate porcelain bowls, 'I realise that you came here in a hurry and that your luggage was necessarily restricted since you came by air. But now I have been thinking that it would give me great pleasure to buy some clothes for you, more suitable perhaps for the life here.'

Maggie flushed. She thought of the way she and Matron had struggled to compile her wardrobe for travelling and she also remembered the words over-heard on her first day here, 'Her clothes are a disaster!'

'It's very kind of you, Sophia, but it's hardly worth my buying new clothes. I'll be here for such a short while and in London I won't need thin dresses. Besides, most of the time I expect to be wearing uniform.'

Sophia frowned and spoke quite sharply.

'It is foolish to be so obstinate and proud, Maggie. Every young girl likes to have new clothes. You can't tell me you like that black dress you wear every evening.'

Tears started to Maggie's eyes. It was true that she did hate the black dress. But if she accepted presents of clothes from Sophia it would be even more difficult to refuse to fall in with her plans for the future.

'It would give me so much pleasure to buy you something pretty and suitable for your age,' Sophia was saying. 'Why won't you give me that joy?'

She was smiling with persuasive charm and Maggie felt she was being ungracious.

'But how would you get clothes for me here?' she asked, clutching at this for an excuse.

'I mentioned it to Stefan and he would be pleased to take you to Windhoek. There is a boutique there which stocks quite good clothes. I will write a letter and tell the proprietor the kind of thing I have in mind, though naturally, my dear child, you must feel free to choose the dresses yourself. I will just list in my letter the kind of dresses you need, so many for day wear, so many for evening and so on. And of course we must include shoes and accessories.'

'But, Baroness, would it be proper for me to go to Windhoek with Stefan alone?' Maggie asked. She was snatching for excuses not to go. Otherwise this would never have occurred to her.

'Boris will go too. I hope that satisfies your ideas of propriety,' said the Baroness, and for a moment Maggie could have sworn she wore the same twinkling expression that Stefan so often had. 'I admire your discretion, Marguerite, and perhaps it is not conventional to go with two men, but after all, this is not a very conventional country, and I am sure you can regard Boris in the place of a parent.'

Sophia paused. 'There is one other thing, Marguerite. Some time ago Stefan became involved with a young woman called Carola de Chantilly. She has been away, but now I understand she has returned. She is most unsuitable for my son, a woman who has been divorced and now has left her second husband. I trust while you are in the town you will do your best to keep Stefan away from her.'

Maggie was startled.

'But, Baroness, good heavens, how can I?'

'You have youth and freshness on your side. You will buy pretty clothes. It is up to you to keep Stefan occupied while you are in town. Make him forget about Carola. What is wrong?' she asked, regarding Maggie's somewhat astonished expression.

'It seems rather a tall order to keep Stefan from someone to whom he is attracted,' said Maggie slowly.

'But I will tell him he must keep you with him, give you a good time while you are in Windhoek. He will feel obliged to be attentive to you when you are his mother's guest. Boris will help you keep him with you.'

That will be delightful, I must say, thought Maggie. I'm to be a watchdog to keep him away from this Carola. What a prospect! And that's probably the only reason he is jumping at the chance to take me to Windhoek, so he can see her. He wasn't over-attentive to his mother's guest the first evening we met. He soon made an excuse to go off to meet Carola.

'For my sake, do your best,' Sophia was saying, smiling with all her considerable charm. 'I love this son of mine very much. I should hate him to make a wrong choice. I had hoped the affair was over when she went to Europe, but now it seems I may be wrong.'

Maggie retired early, for she was stiff and sore from the camel ride.

'Poor old lady,' teased Stefan, when he saw her hobbling up the staircase. 'Would you like me to come to rub you with liniment?'

'Certainly not,' snapped Maggie.

How infuriating she found him. And to think she had had to promise Sophia she would keep him occupied while they were in Windhoek so he would not be able to get involved with Carola. What a hope she had of succeeding! Stefan was the kind of man who always did exactly what he wanted to. And it wasn't very likely he would prefer her company to Carola's, she thought, remembering the glimpse of silver gilt hair and that passionate embrace.

After a hot bath she felt better and had been sleeping for some time in her carved wooden bed when she heard a scratching at the door. 'Go away, Giselle,' she murmured sleepily, for this had happened before. But the scratching became more persistent accompanied by

68

plaintive whines. Maggie, sighing, padded across the stone-flagged floor with feet bare to open the door.

After the heat of the day, the night was chilly. A cold wind was blowing in from the desert, feeling almost as if it was coming from the grey Atlantic one hundred yards away behind the grey dunes. Giselle bounded in, all graceful willowy body and plumy waving tail. Her object was a fur rug that lay beside Maggie's bed and she curled up on this now, very satisfied that her complaints had been answered.

But Maggie, having been disturbed from her first sleep, found it difficult to settle down again. This was strange, for usually she slept soundly. But tonight she felt vaguely worried. She could not understand why this should be except that she did not want to accept Sophia's offer of clothes, because in some way although the Baroness meant it kindly the more she accepted from her the more ungracious she would appear if she did not fall in with the plans for the future.

But there was something else too, something that she could not define, a kind of hurt feeling. But why should she feel hurt? Everyone was being kind to her in their own way, even Stefan. Stefan ... that was it. Something seemed to throb like a physical ache almost like a nagging toothache when she thought of him. But why was that? Surely, Maggie, she admonished herself, you can stand a little teasing? Specially after the kind of upbringing that you had. There was very little scope for injured feelings in your life at the Children's Home.

She drowsed off again, but her sleep seemed doomed to be disturbed that night. Somewhere out in the desert came the eerie 'yip-yip' of a jackal and Giselle, hearing it, was aroused and made restless. She nudged at Maggie and indicated that she wanted to go out again. Maggie stumbled to the door and opened it, but now Giselle refused to move. Except that she finally bounded outside for a few steps and then came back, gazing at Maggie with liquid brown eyes and plainly indicating that she would not go wherever she intended to go without Maggie's company.

'Heavens! What a nuisance you are!' sighed Maggie putting on the Japanese kimono and slippers. But it was difficult to be cross with such a beautiful animal.

'Wherever do you think you're going?' she asked her as the silvery white Giselle led her down the corridor lit with dim cresset lamps and stopped at the door of one of the towers, one that Maggie had not inspected on her tour of the castle. No wonder she had not been willing to come here without Maggie, because obviously she needed someone to open the door.

Maggie hesitated, but she knew that there were no bedrooms in this part of the castle and surely there could be nobody here at this time of night? It was possible that Giselle and Sacha normally slept here so that they would not disturb people. And perhaps Giselle had been shut out by accident this evening. Yes, now she could hear Sacha whining on the other side of the door. That was why Giselle wanted to go there.

She pushed the heavy door and it swung remarkably freely on its hinges. Somehow she had expected it to creak or groan, but it was obviously used and kept oiled. She found herself at the foot of the staircase leading up to the tower room, but found it difficult to move in the narrow space with Sacha and Giselle whirling around her yelping with delirious joy at being reunited.

Suddenly the door to the tower room opened and a

voice reverberated down the stone staircase, 'Sacha, Giselle, what on earth . . .? Why, Maggie, what a pleasant surprise!'

Stefan was standing at the top of the steps and seemed to her fevered imagination to be twelve feet tall. The shadow cast by the lamp he was holding swooped and danced on the wall like a living thing.

'Don't look so startled. When you're surprised your eyes look like two dark moons. Come in. I don't often have a midnight visitor.'

Maggie drew back.

'I'd better go,' she stammered. 'It's late.'

Stefan laughed. His manner to Maggie seemed challenging.

'Do come in and take a look at my study. Surely you're not scared to be alone with me?'

There was a small log fire in the stone fireplace and in front of it was a settee made of red leather, but what drew Maggie's attention was that upon a bench was a large telescope pointed towards the skylight. She forgot all her nervousness and exclaimed, 'Oh, is that yours? How super! I've always wanted to look at the sky through a telescope.'

To Stefan she looked like an eager child.

'So now you can. But not before you tell me why I'm being honoured with a midnight visit.'

It was true, as his mother had said, that Stefan had a wicked smile. But its charm was hard to resist. Maggie found herself smiling too as she replied, 'Giselle brought me. I didn't even know you were here.'

'So I owe your visit not to any interest in me but to Giselle's wifely devotion to Sacha. Too bad! But now you're here I can grant your wish, since you say you've always wanted to look through a telescope. Of course you know that in stories the princess always has to pay a penalty for being granted her heart's desire. Are you willing to pay a penalty, Maggie?' he asked, grinning mischievously.

'Yes, of course.'

Maggie was hardly listening to his chaffing, for he had taken her by the arm and guided her until she was in the best position to scan the heavens.

'Where is the Southern Cross?' she demanded. 'There always seem to be such a lot of them.'

Stefan laughed.

'Don't be impatient. Look for the two pointer stars and there above them you can see the Southern Cross in all its glory. You can find other crosses in the sky, but none as beautiful as that.'

In the dazzling heavens, swinging in the telescope's eye, the bigger stars hung like silver lamps and beyond them million upon million of pinpoints of light receded into space. Maggie felt quite dizzy with this vision of eternity.

'There's Orion's Belt,' Stefan pointed out. His arm was close around her while he manipulated the instrument. 'That's a useful constellation to know if you're lost in the desert. The third star in the middle a little to the right always rises due east and sets due west of you no matter where you may be.'

'But I'm never too sure where east or west are,' Maggie protested.

'You really are a big city girl, aren't you? The Bushmen say that Orion is made up of tortoises hanging upon a stick—I suppose that's because it's specially bright and visible during the spring when tortoises are active here.'

'Do you know lots of Bushman folklore?'

'Quite a lot, because Samgau has told it to me over the camp fire on our hunting expeditions. The Milky Way was made by a girl of ancient race who wished for a little light and threw wood ashes into the sky. Stars were made by throwing scented roots into the air.'

'They must have had to throw an awful lot,' said Maggie, smiling. Above her the Milky Way swung in a large arc crowded with uncountable heavenly bodies.

'There's no moon tonight. That's why you can see the stars so clearly. The Bushmen say that on a moonless night a lion has put his paw over the moon so that it will be dark and he can hunt better.'

Maggie turned to smile at him, but she had not realised he was so close.

'Darling little Maggie,' he said. 'Now I've shown you the stars you must pay the forfeit for getting your wish.'

His mouth came down upon hers in a hard, long kiss. She was so astonished that she did not even try to stop him, but stood still in his arms, bewildered by the strange new sensations that were flowing swift as a river through her mind and body.

Releasing her, he laughed tenderly.

'You really are rather a sweet thing, Maggie. Those pansy brown eyes are going to break someone's heart one day.'

He had kissed her as a woman, but now he was speaking to her as if she were a child. The kiss was just fun to him, the most natural thing in the world when one considered his flirtatious ways.

His arms were around her once more, burning through the thin silk of her kimono, but she drew back hastily.

'I'd better go now, Stefan. It's awfully late.'

He scrutinised her carefully, then frowned.

'You're so young. I haven't made you cross, have I, Maggie? After all, we are almost kissing cousins, remember?'

Maggie shook her head.

'No, I'm not cross, Stefan. Thank you for showing me the stars.'

Hurrying back to her room, she smiled remembering his last words. His kiss had overwhelmed her with feelings she had not known she possessed. But later, lying sleepless, she remembered the young man in the plane. Angus had warned her. It was her own fault if ... But she would not pursue that train of thought. Stefan was right. What's a kiss between friends? she assured herself drowsily.

CHAPTER FIVE

AFTER all the second air journey with Stefan and Boris had been quite pleasant because this time Maggie had taken the precaution of swallowing a tablet to guard against air-sickness. And now she was walking once more along the wide main street, the Kaiserstrasse, trying to match her step to Stefan's long stride.

Boris had gone off on some business of his own concerned with his gemstones and Stefan had suggested that she would need some refreshment before embarking on her shopping expedition, so he had suggested they should have hot chocolate and Viennese tortes at an open-air café close by.

To tell the truth, Maggie was glad of the delay, for she had never shopped on her own for dresses before and the elegant boutique that Stefan had pointed out as the place where she must go was distinctly different from the chain store where she and Matron had bought the cotton frocks. She could have enjoyed being with Stefan in the exhilarating air of this small city if it had not been for the fact that she had to face this ordeal later.

The main street seemed to be becoming modernised, with square new streamlined buildings, but here and there were still the old German houses with their balconies and dormer windows and opposite was a park with tall cypresses and stone pergolas and tiers of flower-beds in containers surrounded by lifelike bronze antelopes.

Stefan must have taken his mother's instructions to heart, for he was being very charming and attentive to her. After they had been served, he pressed her to eat lots of the delicious flaky confections that melted in the mouth, assuring her that he liked to see a girl with a good appetite, and they were laughing together over Maggie's difficulty in making her choice when a shadow fell across the table.

As she looked up at the newcomer, Maggie's vivacity died away. She knew at once it could be none other than Carola, but when she had caught a glimpse of her that other time she had seen only that wonderful silver-gilt hair. Now she encountered the gaze of huge limpid eyes in a most unusual shade of violet blue with a heavy fringe of dark lashes. The mouth was a little full and the nose short and retroussé. In fact the face had the foreshortened look of a Persian cat, but the whole effect was enormously attractive, especially when combined with arms and legs of golden hue emphasised by a pale green wisp of a dress.

'Stefan ... but you did not let me know you were coming. What a pleasant surprise!'

'It was rather a hasty decision. However, here we are. You haven't met Maggie yet, have you?'

Stefan had sprung to his feet, but Carola put her slender hand on his shoulder, pressing him to sit again, and at his persuasion took the other chair herself. Maggie noticed that she was very tall with generous curves very different from Maggie's own small build. She accepted Stefan's offer of a cup of coffee, shuddering delicately when offered the pastries. While she was waiting for a fresh serving of coffee, she surveyed Maggie with frank appraisal.

'So this is Marguerite,' she said in a peculiar tone of

voice. If she had said, 'This is the wonderful Marguerite,' she could not have made her meaning more clear.

'How young she looks! And why do you call her Maggie, Stefan?'

'It's the name she's used to. Don't you think it suits her?'

'Maybe, but it is not a very pretty name.'

Now what did she mean by that? thought Maggie.

'Are you enjoying your stay here?' she asked Maggie.

'Yes, very much,' said Maggie, politely.

'Life at the castle must be quite a change from the mode of life you are used to,' Carola murmured sweetly.

'Yes, it is a bit different from Manchester,' said Maggie flatly.

'What a fascinating accent she has, hasn't she, Stefan?'

'I can't say I had noticed.'

'No? Oh, I think it is too sweet.'

Stefan seemed to brush this aside and turned to their visitor with a persuasive smile.

'Carola, you're just the person we need, isn't she, Maggie? Maman has sent us here with instructions to buy Maggie some clothes. She came away in such a hurry that she didn't have time to get anything suitable. Now you know what kind of things you wear in this climate, so wouldn't it be a good idea if you two girls got together and you can advise Maggie in her choice?'

Stefan was obviously relieved to discard all responsibility for Maggie's purchases and evidently thought it was a brilliant idea to enlist Carola's help. I suppose it is, thought Maggie, trying to conquer her instinctive

77

dislike of the other girl. You're just jealous, she told herself. You've hardly spoken more than two words to her, but just because she's glamorous and well-dressed and because Stefan looks at her with that look in his eyes you have to feel antagonistic to her.

So she meekly accepted Carola's offer of help and Stefan, after he had picked up his car at the hotel, drove them to the boutique promising to call back and take them both to lunch later.

'How odd that you should have left buying clothes until you arrived here,' commented Carola. 'I usually try to buy as many clothes as possible when I visit London. These days it sets fashion more than Paris or Rome, though I always try to get some of those fabulous Italian knits when I'm there. They are gorgeous, don't you agree?'

Maggie was saved a reply because a short rotund lady came forward. She was rather like a pouter pigeon, if one could visualise one dressed in black crêpe. She addressed them in a Continental accent that seemed deliberately exaggerated.

'Madame! What a pleasure to see you! And what can I do for you? You have come just at the right time. I have today received some fabulous imported suits that are just your type.'

'Unfortunately I have not come for clothes for myself, Madame, though I may be tempted to look at them.'

She went into a long explanation in German. Maggie felt very much at a disadvantage because she had not the faintest idea what they were talking about. She stood a little forlornly regarding the small window which displayed an exotic striped slacks suit that she could not imagine herself wearing and a huge canvas

78

bag in orange and purple to match the suit.

'Do you speak German, *Fräulein*?'

'Unfortunately, no.'

'Ah yes, now I remember. I received instructions from the Baroness to let you have a free hand in choosing some clothes. How fortunate you are to have the Baroness for a patron.'

Maggie's proud spirit rebelled at the idea of being regarded as an object of charity, but there was nothing for it. Carola and Madame were looking at her critically as if she fell far short of their usual standards.

'How tiny you are, my dear. I have not much in your size. Madame Carola here has a perfect figure. She can step into practically anything in her size and walk out in it.'

'You flatter me,' smiled Carola.

The two of them went into consultation moving along the racks of clothes and not taking the slightest notice of Maggie. Every now and again they picked out a dress or a suit. At first Madame seemed inclined to argue over Carola's choice, but she was quickly reconciled by the fact that the clothes chosen were amongst the most expensive in her stock.

Maggie tried to tag along and every now and again catching a glimpse of something they had taken out, said, 'Isn't that a bit fancy?' But she was overruled by the other two who assured her that what they were choosing was the latest fashion. When finally she reached the cubicle and started trying on the clothes she was amazed to find that Carola had picked out clothes that she felt sure she would never have chosen for herself, clothes that were made in large bright patterns or were heavily beaded.

As she started trying them on she felt quite desperate. What made it worse was that Madame seemed determined to sell her the clothes without really minding whether they were suited to her. She felt quite dizzy with her perpetual flow of conversation. 'Now this is beautiful. Just feel the quality. Of course these are imported from Paris. See the perfect beadwork.'

She was aided and abetted by Carola, who kept assuring Maggie she looked charming in everything. The worse Maggie felt in a dress the more Carola seemed to be enchanted with it. Maggie, who was not used to choosing clothes, felt utterly bewildered. Was she wrong? Was this the kind of thing she should be wearing? She thought of Sophia saying, 'Her clothes are a disaster!' Certainly she had never had much chance to cultivate good taste in clothes, but surely these kind were not what Sophia had intended her to buy.

'Haven't you anything simpler?' she asked Madame, when she had struggled in and out of a shining emerald green lurex garment that made her look, she thought, like a string bean.

'Simpler? But these are the very latest. The Baroness would wish me to give you the best clothes I have in stock.'

Maggie surprised a sly smile on Carola's face. She's doing this on purpose, she thought, with a sudden revelation. She wants me to look overdressed and stupid and to spend far too much money on unsuitable clothes.

Madame was piling up the clothes, saying, 'You will be taking this, of course, and this, and you looked charming in this ... didn't she, Madame Carola?'

'Oh yes, delightful,' agreed Carola, all smiles.

Maggie spoke in the voice she used when she was

quelling the younger orphans when they were throwing water in the showers, a level determined manner that brooked very little opposition.

'I'm sorry, Madame, for the trouble you have taken, but I won't be buying any of these.'

There was a stunned silence. Maggie could have laughed at the change if she had not been feeling so upset.

'But, *Fräulein*, how can you say that? These clothes are beautiful, the best in the city.'

'They may be, said Maggie flatly, her north-country accent more pronounced. 'But I just don't fancy them. I'm sorry you've wasted your time on me, but there it is. I will make do with what I've got.'

The look Madame gave to the brown-and-white-striped dress showed clearly what she thought of it.

'But I don't understand. Have I done something to annoy the *Fräulein*?'

'Not a thing,' said Maggie, feeling a qualm of dismay because the woman looked so perturbed and it was not really her fault. 'But I'm only staying here a month, and these clothes are not suitable for the life I'll be leading after that. They're beautifully made, as you say, but not for me.'

Carola had been listening to this conversation without interfering, but now her eyes seemed to go a deeper violet and she tossed her head, reminding Maggie in some way of a Persian cat that has been deprived of its mouse.

'How can you be so absurd, Maggie? If you go back to the castle without having bought any clothes, Sophia is going to be dreadfully hurt. For heaven's sake! Most girls would give their souls to have such expensive garments, and as Madame says, they are the very latest imports.'

'I don't fancy them,' Maggie repeated obstinately.

The shop bell rang and Stefan's voice shouted, 'How's it going? Have you nearly finished? I'm expecting Maggie to have bought the whole shop.'

But when he saw them emerging from the cubicle, he realised something was wrong. Carola's eyes were flashing in spite of the charming smile she produced for Stefan, Madame's expression was thunderous, and Maggie looked like a kitten surrounded by barking dogs.

'I'm afraid we have wasted Madame's time,' explained Carola. 'Maggie does not like the clothes one can buy here. It is a pity she did not equip herself better in London.'

'Oh, for God's sake, Maggie, what nonsense is this? I promised Maman I would bring you back with some new clothes and I'm going to do it,' vowed Stefan. 'Leave us, Carola. Drive to the hotel and then send the car back for us in half an hour. We'll all meet for lunch.'

Carola shrugged her shoulders and flounced out of the shop.

'Now let's see what you've been trying, Maggie.'

Maggie's small face set in determined lines.

'You aren't going to persuade me I look nice in them, Stefan, because I don't.'

She was having a hard task to keep the tears from her eyes. His anger was the last straw after her ordeal with Madame and Carola.

'What an obstinate little creature you are!' Then, as she gulped, 'Now, for God's sake, I can't stand tears. Madame, show me what you've been trying to sell her.'

But when he saw the collection of clothes still lying in the fitting-room his comment was 'Oh Golly!' and Maggie could not help smiling through her tears at his expression.

'How could you think this kind of thing would suit a young girl?' he demanded of Madame.

'Herr von Linsingen, I keep only the best in my boutique. If the *Fräulein* is not pleased ...' Madame bridled, but Stefan was visibly unimpressed by her manner.

'Madame de Chantilly assured me that this was the kind of garment the *Fräulein* wanted. Certainly I do not keep cheap clothes in my boutique.'

'It may be what she wanted, but if they did not suit her when she tried them on it would have been foolish of her to buy them. Put these all away and we will start over again.'

He swept along the racks, swiftly picking out more dresses, simple well-cut clothes that Maggie had not even been shown before.

'What colours do you like, Maggie? Turquoise, pink, green? Rose pink would suit those brown eyes. Try them on now and be quick. I'm hungry. I want my lunch.'

In no time at all he had chosen half a dozen pretty day dresses for her and a couple of evening gowns as well as slacks, shirts and all the accessories needed. Madame was quite different now, all eagerness to please.

'Now no more nonsense, Maggie,' Stefan admonished her. 'You must have what I chose. You look great in those.'

This time Maggie did not protest. Although she was rather amazed by his high-handed handling of the situation, she was quite happy with his choice of clothes.

But when they were in the car driving to the delayed lunch, Stefan said, 'What on earth made you think you could wear such fancy clothes, Maggie? Why did you pick them out in the first place?'

'I didn't, really, it was just...'

How could she say that Carola tried to make her buy the wrong kind of clothes?

'That kind of thing may be all right for someone like Carola who's tall and striking and can carry it off, but not for you, Maggie. You shouldn't try to be spectacular.'

'No, I don't suppose I should,' said Maggie, feeling strangely dampened by his frank statement.

Boris joined them for lunch accompanied by Angus who seemed pleased to see Maggie again. While Carola monopolised Stefan to the exclusion of everyone else, Boris and Angus kept Maggie entertained with stories of their expeditions for gemstones.

'We are going to Usakos tomorrow to see if we can get any tourmaline,' Boris said. 'How about coming with us, Marguerite?'

Maggie looked questioningly at Stefan, but he was deep in conversation with Carola. She had her hand on his arm and was gazing at him with those wonderful violet eyes.

'How about it, Stefan?' said Boris, interrupting what looked like a very intimate scene. 'Can we take Marguerite with us on our rock hunting tomorrow? What are your plans?'

'I had thought we could go to Swakopmund for tomorrow and the next day to show Maggie a bit of the coastline. The villa is always prepared and the servants are there. We can send them a wire to expect us. Carola

84

here might consent to act as chaperon. Would you, Carola?'

'Certainly,' said Carola, shrugging her shoulders and not looking too pleased at this remark. 'If you think I am old enough to fulfil such a role.'

'You can chaperon each other,' said Stefan. 'Usakos is en route for Swakopmund. You, Boris and Angus, can take another car and I will take the girls on ahead.'

Maggie was rather sorry about this arrangement. It meant that she would be an unwilling third accompanying Stefan and Carola, but she had reluctantly promised Sophia she would act as watchdog, so she supposed she had better not object.

But there was nothing she could do about this afternoon. Carola blatantly commandeered Stefan, saying she must have his company in a drive she had to take to see some friends in the Khomas Hoogland, the hilly country beyond the city. She did not offer to take anyone else, but Stefan turned and said, 'How about Maggie? Shouldn't we take her with us?'

The expression on Carola's face made Maggie want to laugh and she replied quickly, 'No, thank you, Angus is taking me on a tour of the town.'

Angus looked a little surprised but pleased as well.

'Aye,' he affirmed, catching on to her scheme with gratifying fervour. 'Miss Young ... Maggie is coming with me. It will be a pleasure to show her the Tintenpalast and the old fort and the castle and the cemetery.'

'The cemetery?' asked Maggie, somewhat startled.

'Oh aye, everyone who comes to Windhoek must see the cemetery. It's one of the prettiest places in town for a stroll because it has hedges and rose gardens and avenues of trees, and these are a bit rare in a country the likes of this.'

Stefan did not look very pleased and Maggie remembered Angus had said they had been at cross-purposes occasionally. But she could not help that, she thought defiantly. Besides, in spite of what Sophia had said she was not going to play gooseberry to Stefan and Carola more than she could help.

'Look, you don't have to take me around,' explained Maggie, as soon as they were out of earshot and on their way to Angus's car.

'I will be verra pleased to show you the town,' Angus assured her, his Scottish burr more pronounced than ever. 'I would have suggested it myself, but I thought...' It was plain what he had thought, that Maggie would be going with Stefan.

'I didn't want to intrude on them,' explained Maggie.

'No, better not,' Angus agreed. 'She's a bonny lassie. Got a strong personality, too, I hear, but Stefan will be able to manage her. When it comes to strong wills I reckon they're two of a kind.'

Maggie changed the subject by asking something about the town. She felt she did not want to discuss Stefan's matrimonial prospects. Sophia might disapprove, but it seemed to be taken for granted that Carola and Stefan were intended for each other. So why should she feel depressed about it? In a month's time she would be back in London and could safely forget about all these rather exotic people.

Wherever you went in Windhoek the long double-storeyed Administration Building, nicknamed the Palace of Ink, dominated the scene, standing as it did on a rise overlooking the town. Angus took Maggie into the gardens where he showed her the collection of strange plants that grow in South West Africa. There were desert succulents like stones and at the other extreme, tropical palms that normally grow in the north amongst the palm groves and forest and plains of Ovamboland. But the strangest plant on exhibition was the Welwischia Mirabilis.

'The specimens here are not very wonderful. It grows only in certain parts of the country,' Angus explained. 'It often looks like an untidy heap of huge tattered dead leaves, but at its best it has blue-green leaves and light red cones or brilliant orange ones.'

'How does it get water in the desert?' asked Maggie.

'The taproot goes down sometimes to sixty feet to find water from old river-beds. It belongs to the pine family, though you wouldn't think so, would you, except for the cones? Some people call it the desert octopus, for in the desert the great twelve-foot leaves get torn into papery strands by the wind and look as if they're crawling over the sand.'

'I'd like to see it in its natural surroundings,' said Maggie.

'Maybe I can take you one day,' exclaimed Angus, and then looked confused. It was unlike him to be so impulsive.

'That's nice of you,' said Maggie tactfully. 'But I'm only staying for a little while, I think.'

'And nae doot you have lots to do while you are here,' Angus agreed.

How quickly he withdraws into his shell, thought Maggie, and she set herself to be nice to this rather shy young man as he took her around Windhoek, to the cemetery which really was beautiful, to the zoo garden, where he explained about the collection of meteorites in a very knowledgeable way, to the old fort standing on a hill and to the romantic castles each standing on their own hillock overlooking the town, each one bringing an atmosphere of the Rhineland to this hot African country.

Maggie enjoyed the afternoon with Angus even though every now and again she could not help thinking of those two others, Stefan whose leonine good looks matched so well the feminine beauty of Carola with her silver-gilt hair and fascinating violet eyes, driving through the lovely mountainous region above Windhoek. They're so well suited, she thought. I wonder why Sophia is so much against Carola? I suppose it's that she doesn't like her having been divorced.

'Boris has asked me to join him for dinner,' said Angus when they parted. 'Will I be seeing you there, this evening?'

'Yes, I expect so,' Maggie replied.

When she went to her room the parcel of dresses had arrived from the shop and she eagerly lifted the lid. Never before had she had the thrill of owning so many lovely clothes. And all at once! But would she do them justice? She remembered she had noticed a beauty salon connected with the hotel, and now she conquered her shyness and phoned the reception desk to ask if she could get her hair set at this rather late hour.

Soon her golden-brown hair was enhanced by a colour rinse and curling in silky fronds around her neat small head, and she had purchased some flattering peach-coloured brush-on make-up, coral lipstick, turquoise eye-shadow and dark brown mascara. When, after a leisurely bath, she had used these aids to beauty and slipped into the sleeveless golden yellow dress with its slim lines and scooped neck and put on the new bronze sandals, she was surprised at her own reflection.

When she went downstairs, Boris and Angus were sitting in the open courtyard having a drink together, but when he saw Maggie, Boris sprang up and said 'What a pretty dress, Marguerite! If they all make you look as charming as this, Sophia will think you have chosen well, don't you think so, Angus?'

Angus, who had also risen, looked at her appreciatively.

'Aye, she looks bonny,' he agreed.

There could not be a greater contrast, thought Maggie, between the charming very Continental older man expressing his feelings with generous gestures and the rather serious Scot, who was regarding her with a shy smile, but they both seemed to agree that she was looking particularly nice in her new dress. She wondered if Stefan would notice. It seemed very important that he should like her appearance too. He should do because it was he who had chosen the dress. But he had done it in a tearing hurry, not really caring whether Maggie looked attractive in them or not, just so long as he got something that was not exaggerated.

However, when Stefan eventually did arrive with Carola, she found his astonishment rather embarrassing. His eyes danced when he saw her sitting there so demurely in her yellow dress with her hair that looked like a bronze chrysanthemum.

'Let me have a proper look at you, Maggie,' he demanded, and whisked her up on to her feet, turning her around so he could see her at all angles.

'My, my, doesn't she look a sweetie?' he asked the assembled company. 'Who would have thought my little Maggie could look such a honey?'

He hugged her as one would hug a child and turned to Carola, saying, 'You see, Carola, all you needed was a little firmness. You shouldn't have let Maggie persuade you she needed such fancy clothes.'

Somehow Carola must have twisted this morning's events to her own advantage. She had evidently told Stefan that the elaborate clothes were Maggie's choice and that when she had tried to persuade her to choose something different Maggie had decided she did not want any.

She herself was wearing a very sophisticated black crêpe dress held upon the shoulders by two slender diamanté straps. She looked with disfavour upon Boris, Angus and Maggie and said, pouting and loud enough to be heard, 'I thought we had decided to spend the evening alone together, Stefan darling.'

'Later, darling,' said Stefan rather indifferently. 'The night is young. First I had thought we would show Maggie a Bavarian evening.'

'Oh no, Stefan, they're really too hearty for my taste.'

'Just for once, Carola, to please me ... and Maggie, of course. We'll only go for a little while. We can eat there too.'

'If you like beer and German sausages,' said Carola, shrugging her lovely shoulders.

In spite of the other girl's objections, Stefan overruled her, and Maggie found herself in a replica of a German beer hall with old-world wooden tables and benches, and pink-cheeked waitresses dressed in Tyrolean costume of white blouses with puffed sleeves, green waistcoats with silver buttons, dirndls braided with black and black shoes with silver buckles.

As they were eating substantial plates of sausage and sauerkraut, accompanied in the men's case by large tankards of light German lager, Maggie watched fascinated as the German band played an accompaniment to some expert folk-dancing. Dust rose from the floor with these strenuous exertions and a group of men surrounded the band with raised tankards and almost raised the rafters with the song, 'Trink, trink, Bruderlein, trink.'

'Will you dance with me, Maggie?' asked Stefan, when this was over and the dancing had become general, 'I know Carola won't condescend to join in this kind of thing.'

Maggie, who had been watching the dancing rather enviously, sprang up and Stefan whirled her away in a mad spinning movement. She felt so carefree, so lighthearted. What did it matter if Carola was frowning? It was such fun dancing with Stefan. All the dancers looked gay, laughing and smiling at each other, and those who were not dancing raised their voices in hearty chorus.

Afterwards when Maggie had had time to recover her breath, Angus asked if she would care to dance with him. To Maggie's surprise, for he was a rather stiff young man, he was very light on his feet. This came, he told her when she complimented him, from doing Highland dancing when he was a boy. Once or twice as they whirled near to their table she noticed that Carola and Stefan seemed to be talking together with great vehemence on her part, but she was so busy following the steps that she did not give much thought to it.

When they came back to sit at the table, however, Carola smiled sweetly at Maggie, saying, 'Isn't it amazing? It's the first time I have known Stefan to have brotherly feelings for a girl. He says you have had enough exertion for one day and refuses to take us on to a nightclub. I told him that in any case you are enjoying yourself so much with Angus that obviously you would not mind staying here while we go on.'

Maggie felt sure Carola expected that she would agree wholeheartedly to Carola and Stefan going to the nightclub by themselves, but, remembering Sophia's request to her to keep an eye on Stefan, she said, 'But of course, I would be delighted to go on to a nightclub.'

Carola looked furious that her scheme had gone awry, and soon they were all seated in a rather crowded smoky room with a postage-stamp-sized floor for dancing. While Boris ordered a light white wine, Carola put persuasive golden arms around Stefan's neck and led him off to dance. It was a rather different style from the gay Bavarian folk-dancing, thought Maggie.

'I'm afraid I'm not so good at this,' Angus apologised as they sat at the table watching the couples barely moving on the crowded floor. Maggie did not mind. It was one thing to caper around the floor as she had done at the other place, but quite another to sway in a close embrace to the sensuous sweetly shrill strains of a saxaphone solo. She was not at all sure that she would like it.

It did not seem long, however, before Stefan and Carola were back at the table, Carola looking distinctly ruffled and making some audible remark about this baby-sitting was being carried too far. Stefan, taking no notice of this at all, asked Maggie if she would like to dance.

When he held her in his arms, she was astonished by her own feeling of warm response. This was different from the gay vivacity of their Bavarian dance. The dark shadowed face above her seemed that of a stranger, grave and brooding. What was he thinking of as he held her so close amongst the swaying crowd, so hemmed in by the other dancers and yet so entirely alone?

The blonde vocalist took hold of the microphone, giving all her soul to an old torch song, 'Some day he'll come along, the man I love . . .' Was it her imagination or had the dark face above her softened into a tender smile?

There in the stuffy crowded room, surrounded by people, some raucous, some a little drunk, like a flash of lightning the overwhelming idea came, 'It's too late to think about your warnings now, Angus. I'm falling in love with him. Oh, my goodness, how crazy, how completely mad!'

She was glad it was so dark in the nightclub. Perhaps by the time they got back to their table with its faint candlelight she could regain her composure. Meanwhile neither of them had spoken. The astonishing revelation had come to her with not a word exchanged. Was it possible that only she was feeling this overwhelming emotion? Could it not have touched him at all?

She ventured another glance. He was smiling and his arm tightened around her waist. 'Do you know how sweet you are, Maggie, my love?' he murmured, his lips against her hair. She smiled in a bemused way, for once all her quick witty responses with him forgotten. But he had said that kind of thing before. How could one know whether he was ever serious? Maggie admonished herself that she must try to be sensible, but how could she when all the time she was so filled with indescribable bliss?

'Home now,' he said firmly, when they returned to the table. 'We must all get a little sleep before our journey tomorrow.'

93

Carola, who had been dancing with Boris, flashed a look of dislike at Maggie, who was immediately conscious that Stefan still had his arm around her waist and did not seem to be making any effort to disengage it.

Driving back to the hotel, Carola placed herself with a determined air in the front passenger seat and Maggie found herself between Angus and Boris in the back. An enormous silver moon was rising over the distant Auas mountains, shining on the old German houses and giving an ethereal quality to the scene. To Maggie it looked unreal, and the turmoil of her thoughts seemed equally so. Perhaps tomorrow she would awake and this would all seem like a dream.

CHAPTER SIX

BUT next morning the feeling of enchantment remained. She was awakened before dawn by a servant with a cup of coffee and a small plate of rusks. Dunking them in the hot sweet brew as she had learned to do since she came to Africa, she felt a thrilling excitement that before her lay a whole wonderful day of new experiences to be had with Stefan at her side.

She admonished herself not to be stupid, for of course Carola would be there too, Carola with her glorious silver-gilt hair and those large violet eyes that could gaze so limpidly into Stefan's stormy grey ones.

This morning Maggie wore the short French navy pleated skirt and red and white tunic top that was one of the outfits Stefan had picked out yesterday. The red and white canvas sneakers that went with it were suitable for a day in the country, she thought.

When she arrived at the open place where the cars were parked, there seemed to be some kind of an argument taking place between Stefan and Carola, glamorous even at this early hour in a figure-hugging slacks suit of clinging white material and a long ultramarine scarf.

'But, Stefan darling,' she heard Carola say, 'I am sure Maggie would prefer to go with Angus and Boris. Surely you noticed how well she was getting on with our young Scotsman last night?'

'All the more reason that she should come with us, then,' replied Stefan adamantly. 'After all, she is in my care while she's away from Maman. She's so young. I can't let any Tom, Dick or Harry start taking an interest in her. And Boris won't be much use. He's too concerned with getting his rocks.'

Carola gave a silvery trill of laughter.

'That I should live to see you pretending to be a watchdog! Can it be that you are just a teeny-weeny bit jealous when a girl even as homely as our Maggie shows an interest in anyone else but your lordship? Really, Stefan, how can you be so obvious? But here comes Maggie herself. Let's put it to her.'

They did not seem to realise how their voices had carried in the clear still morning air.

'Put what to me?' asked Maggie a little sharply. She was still smarting at the phrase 'as homely as our Maggie'.

'I was saying to Stefan that I am sure you would prefer the company of Boris and wee Angus to ours today. The lapidary's place at Usakos is positively fascinating, and of course afterwards you will rejoin us at the villa. Why should she miss seeing all those lovely gems, Stefan?'

'Why, indeed?' said Stefan. His eyes were at their most grey and stormy and he seemed a different person from the one who had shared those precious moments on the crowded dance floor. 'Why should any of us miss it? We will all go together in the Mercedes. It won't take Boris long to choose his stones, and after all, we are making a very early start.'

Maggie could not help giving a smile of joy. It would be much more enjoyable doing the journey this way. She had been dreading being the odd girl out in the other car. But why ever had Stefan suggested it? Perhaps he did not like Carola to get too much of her own

96

way. She was looking positively furious at this turn of events.

'Poor Maggie,' she murmured sympathetically, 'I am quite sure she would have preferred Angus's company to ours today. Specially since they seemed to get on so well from the start.'

Maggie wondered blankly why Carola seemed determined to promote this mythical interest in Angus, when really she had never shown any interest in him. It was quite true he was a thoroughly nice young man, but certainly not very exciting. And since when did you want young men to be exciting? she seemed to hear Matron admonishing her. Since I met Stefan, she heard herself reply to this shadowy figure from her immediate past.

As they reached the plateau above the still sleeping town and began to drive through the uplands, the country unfolding before them was dark blue in the shadows upon the distant hills, peach pink where the sun was gradually reaching the higher land. How attractive this farming country was, thought Maggie. A gentle breeze played over the waving grass that shone silver green as it was set in motion like the restless waves of the sea. Flat thorn trees cast deep ultramarine shadows on the earth beneath, but it was not yet hot enough for the cattle to seek their protection.

Reaching Usakos, they had a meal at one of the hotels before going in search of Boris's lapidary. The small town that owed its existence to the fact that it had been a railway junction and mining centre was something like a place in a Wild West tale with its sandy streets and stores full of varied goods. The hotel was crowded with all kinds of people.

As Boris explained, it was a stopping place before

people set out to cross the Namib desert. They dropped in here for a meal, a drink, for petrol and supplies, and in the case of commercial travellers to display their wares, something like the old-fashioned pedlars used to do, but of course with much more sophisticated goods.

Maggie would have liked to linger for a while watching the tall Herero women in their colourful Victorian costumes and the varied assortment of Africans and coloured people congregating under the straggly pepper trees near the hotel, but Boris was impatient to accomplish his errand and Carola urged her rather sharply to hurry and stop dreaming. Stefan laughed. Carola's remarks, instead of drawing his attention to Maggie's shortcomings, seemed to have aroused his interest.

'She is a dreamer, isn't she, in spite of that so practical streak. What's the meaning of that far-away look in your eyes, Maggie? Have you ever noticed what beautiful eyes the child has, Boris?' he demanded.

'Naturally,' Boris responded. 'Pure topaz, aren't they, Marguerite?'

Maggie, somewhat embarrassed by all this attention, surprised a look of keen dislike in Carola's expression.

'And what are Carola's?' she demanded hastily.

'Lapis lazuli,' Boris answered. 'Even to the tiny gold flecks in them.'

But still Carola did not look pleased. It would have been more welcome if the compliment had come from Stefan, Maggie surmised. She was used to being the centre of attention and seemed to resent the men's interest in the other girl. In this setting, Maggie's fresh youthfulness and vivid interest in her novel surroundings was quite as intriguing to her companions as the

98

charms of the more beautiful woman. But she did not realise this. She only knew that the men were all being very kind of her and that she was very happy in their company and looking forward to the whole trip in spite of Carola's unfriendly attitude.

At the lapidary's Boris and Angus were welcomed as old friends. As Carola had said, it really was a fascinating place. In the Erongo mountains around Usakos there were many deposits of minerals that could be used for making the jewellery so much in demand now by tourists to Southern Africa. It seemed odd to Maggie that these beautiful gems should be known as semi-precious stones, for they looked very precious to her, and indeed some of them, when well cut, were worth a great deal of money.

All kinds of stones were to be found in the Usakos district, yellow topaz, white topaz, smoky and silver topaz, beryl, green, violet, red, white and black tourmaline, tiger-eye, aquamarines, heliodores and numerous others. There was a wonderful collection to be seen here and they had been polished with the utmost skill. The man who kept this collection allowed Boris to purchase some of the uncut stone.

'It's much more fun, of course, retrieving the rock oneself, but unfortunately we haven't much time. But before Maggie goes we must have a gem-finding expedition, what do you think, Stefan? We could combine it with looking at Bushman paintings.'

Stefan purchased a tiger-eye bracelet for Maggie and one of uncut amethyst for Carola.

'Not quite as luxurious as topaz and lapis lazuli, but they do match your eyes,' he assured them. The fascinating golden yellow of the tiger-eye bracelet certainly did have the same warm golden brown as Maggie's and the amethyst bracelet was of a deep violet colour.

The last part of their journey was along the road traversing the Namib desert. Maggie had heard so much about this dread place that now she was astonished to find it was not as grim as she had imagined. It seemed so colourful, so alive with ever-changing scenery as it rolled out in front of them, beside the monotonous road. Sometimes there were great outcrops of basalt and quartz rocks and high yellow sand dunes and always on the right was the Spitzkopje, the mountain with its extraordinary sharp points, visible for miles around.

Maggie was charmed by the desert's subtle colouring, its yellow and browns and reds near at hand with blues and purples in the distance.

'But look—you said there wasn't any water here, and there's a lake!' she exclaimed suddenly, then felt confused as Stefan laughed and explained that it was a mirage. It disappeared as they approached, but then later there was a whole chain of lakes that reflected distant mountaintops. It was all rather bewildering.

And when they approached Swakopmund that in its turn seemed equally unreal.

'How pretty, but it looks like a film set,' exclaimed Maggie.

Its charm lay in its old-world buildings, as if one had transported an old German town to sit on the edge of the sandy desert, and yet on its other side to be washed by the grey waves of the cold Atlantic sea. On the right of the railway line as they drove into the town there was a very palatial-looking building like a superior kind of chalet with a half-timbered front.

'Would you like to stay at that hotel, Maggie?' asked Stefan.

'Why, yes, but I thought...' She meant there had been talk of staying in a villa. 'It looks a very picturesque hotel,' she assured him in case he thought she was quibbling. The men all burst out laughing and she looked at them in some bewilderment.

'It's Stefan's idea of a joke,' explained Carola, her tone acid. 'Rather a corny one, however. Stefan, I promise you I will scream if you ever pull that one again.'

'Sorry, Carola darling, but it always works. That's the local gaol,' he explained to Maggie. 'Isn't it pretty?'

She found in fact that they were to stay at one of the attractive small villas built in the German style with towers and turrets which gave to it an intriguing odd shape. They looked a little too elaborate for a hot climate and yet the high ceilings and thick walls together with the small windows gave a delightfully cool atmosphere.

Another Herero woman, who was Serafina's sister, was housekeeper here and there was an African man-servant too. Everything was in readiness and in a few seconds jugs of hot water were brought to the spacious bedrooms. In a short time, Stefan knocked at the door of Maggie's room and, without waiting for her to open it, shouted, 'I'll give you fifteen minutes to tidy up, Maggie, and then I want to show you the town.'

The water the maid had supplied was rather *brak* as they seemed to call it here in Africa, that is to say it was rather hard and salty. But after using it Maggie felt refreshed and changed into a tobacco-brown slacks suit for the wind blowing through the window from the sea was cool after the heat of the desert journey.

Stefan was alone in the cool whitewashed living-room when Maggie rejoined him. What had happened to Carola? she wondered.

'Carola has dashed off to the hairdresser's,' Stefan explained. 'She says she must get the dust of the Namib out of her hair.'

Maggie, who had worn a silk scarf during the journey, had protected her precious set from too much dust, but she also had been forced to deal with the havoc of the insidious sand by brushing her hair vigorously and applying lemon verbena cologne. And after that there was not much left of last night's glamorous appearance, she noted regretfully. The streets of the little town were of sand bound with salt and some still had the old sidewalks made of wooden boards. As one walked they made a characteristic sound, 'voim ... voim ...'

In creating this holiday resort lying between the sea and the desert, air-conditioned by the cold Atlantic even in the hottest months, the old German colonists had made something quite unique. With its turrets and odd-shaped half-timbered buildings, one almost expected to be able to see snow-capped mountains behind it. It was like a bit of Rhineland set down on this wild barren coast.

A feeling of dreamlike happiness came to Maggie as she walked with Stefan along the sea-front towards the jetty. He had tucked her arm protectively in his and she tried to match her step to his long stride. He showed her the Namib gardens on the esplanade and she marvelled at the immense amount of work that must have taken place to create this lovely spot which even had trees under which one could sit.

'The residents here have been able to create beauty out of the wilderness because Swakopmund is protected from the sand storms by its position on the north side of the river. They can make gardens here, unlike Walvis Bay which is constantly battered by sand,' explained Stefan. 'There's a saying about Walvis Bay that God is ashamed of having made it and that every day He tries to cover it up with sand.'

Maggie laughed, but she hardly heard what he was saying. She was only conscious that she was here with him in this odd exotic little town and that he seemed to seek out her company however 'homely' Carola might think her.

They walked past the stone mole, relic of an abandoned attempt to make a harbour, and south of this found a long wooden jetty.

'Here's where we'll get the best view of the town,' said Stefan, and led her past the few anglers to the end from where they could look back. Distance lent still more enchantment to the toy-like buildings spread out along the sea-front, and north and east was the setting of flat white desert with the sharp edges of sand-dunes in the south stretching away to the pastel green of the evening sky. In front of them the cold-looking dark grey waves pounded up the steep sloping beaches.

Stefan's arm was protectively around her as they stood there beside the darkening sea.

'An exquisitely pretty seaside resort, isn't it?' he asked. 'But on the cruellest coast in the world.'

'Where have you two been hiding?' asked Boris, when they arrived back at the villa. 'Angus and I have been to the hotel and discovered that a four-piece band from Vienna is to perform tonight. I have booked a table for dinner. It should be good fun.'

Maggie decided to wear a white dress this evening which, to offset its simple lines, had a gold chain belt and gold sandals. She brushed out her straight hair, noting with satisfaction that it still retained a bouncy swirl at the ends, and tied it back with a wide white band.

She was pleased with her appearance until she saw Carola in a shimmering dress of a shade between violet and blue, with her hair upswept in a highly sophisticated style. Then Maggie felt she looked about sixteen, which opinion was confirmed by Boris, who said admiringly, 'Marguerite, you look like your namesake, as young as a daisy in spring.'

'Yes, indeed, our Maggie looks so sweet,' purred Carola, her eyes colder than her smile. 'I suppose you always wore white on Sundays where you came from, Maggie? Rather clever of you to do it up with gold.'

Maggie knew that the simple dress had cost Sophia more than she would ever have dreamed of paying herself, so was extremely nettled, as Carola had intended she should be.

'The difference was,' she said, 'that our church dresses had to have long sleeves. It must be a long time since you went to school, Carola, if you think this is a Sunday School dress.'

Stefan, who had missed this little interchange, came clattering down the wooden stairs into the living room of the villa. He had changed into dark close-fitting slacks with a white shirt and red cravat and the golden brown of his tanned skin was even more conspicuous than usual.

'Am I well-dressed enough to take two lovely ladies out to dine?' he asked, putting his arms around both their waists and hugging them close.

'Don't forget, please, that we are coming too,' Boris protested. 'You can't monopolise them even if you have the advantage of youth. I can still do a Viennese waltz, I hope.'

'Probably much better than I can,' agreed Stefan, releasing them as Angus arrived.

'If youth is anything to go by I should have thought Angus had all the advantage,' said Carola silkily. 'He is much nearer Maggie's age than either you or Boris.'

'Thanks for reminding me,' snapped Stefan, but he was only temporarily disconcerted by Carola's tart remark. Almost immediately he drew Maggie to the open window and started pointing out to her the curving line of lights on the foreshore. With his arm on her shoulder, Maggie listened to the soft swish-swish of the waves which had darkened with the night to steely grey. 'Stefan, Stefan, Stefan,' they seemed to be saying to her. She had completely forgotten that there was anyone else in the room and was quite startled when Carola snapped, 'Well, hadn't we better go if we want to make sure of our table?'

The whole town, residents and visitors alike, had turned out to welcome the Viennese orchestra. At first they had all been content to sit and listen to them, while drinking the '*bowle*', a kind of punch, fragrant with pineapple and wine. But after the buffet supper of cold meats and salads, the dancing started and soon the crowded dance floor was covered with whirling couples.

Carola had made a determined effort to keep Stefan at her side this evening and it seemed she was succeeding, or was it just that it accorded with his own wishes? Maggie was left to take it in turns to waltz with Boris and Angus. A few days ago she would have enjoyed this, but tonight her eyes followed the tawny head that towered above all others in the crowded room. She tried not to notice too much that Carola had one slender hand caressingly around Stefan's neck and was gazing up into his eyes with a melting tender expression in those large hyacinth eyes.

She saw with dismay that Carola drew Stefan into joining a crowd of lighthearted guests who seemed to be disposing of a great deal of champagne in a very short time. Soon their laughter became so loud that it overshadowed the light sweet sounds of the quartet and, when a solo was announced, some of the men annoyed other guests by shouting comments as the singer performed.

Boris, whose manners were formal and courteous in the extreme, frowned with irritation, but Angus, ignoring the scene, asked Maggie to dance as if he were quite oblivious of the fact that the other two of their party had deserted them. Maggie, however, scarcely noticed Angus's laboured conversation, though he was making a great effort to be talkative, and that was quite a feat or him. For the first time in his serious life he found himself attracted to a girl and he tried in vain to bring a smile to her lips as they swung around the dance floor.

It was foolish of her, thought Maggie, to have expected so much from this evening. Just because Stefan had paid her a little attention it did not mean that she should have expected him to dance with her. But the music was lovely! If only . . . if only she was in his arms, waltzing and waltzing to the old-fashioned romantic tunes. His grey eyes would be smiling, not dark and clouded as she had seen them on occasion. But tonight his smiles were all for Carola and their own particular set of friends.

She looked around the room, not able to resist the

temptation of looking at him even if the sight of him with Carola was like a knife-thrust to the heart. But they seemed to have disappeared. She felt as if she could no longer make the effort to dance, and, making some excuse about wanting fresh air, she said, 'Let's go outside for a moment, shall we?'

Angus was glad enough to have Maggie's company to himself and they strolled along the sea-front. In the clear moonlight the German architecture of the little town made it look like a scene from a fairy story.

'I understand that you get the best view of the town from the jetty,' said Angus. 'Do you feel up to walking as far as that? It's no so far really.'

Only this afternoon, Maggie had felt so happy while standing here with Stefan. And now in the moonlight the view looked even more romantic with the little white town spread along the sea-front and the path of light bright over the water. But she was with the wrong man.

Why had she committed herself to this heartache? Obviously Stefan was not in the least interested in her. When Angus put his arm around her on the way back ostensibly to protect her from the chill wind, she did not discourage him, for it made her feel a little more secure and wanted. It was thus that Stefan found them when he came striding out of the hotel in search of her, closely followed by Carola.

'For God's sake, Maggie, where have you been? We've been searching the place for you!'

'I hadn't noticed it,' retorted Maggie coldly.

She was embarrassed at being found with Angus in a situation that seemed to confirm Carola's insinuations, but she was also angry at the accusing tone Stefan was using when for the whole evening previously he had ignored her.

'What on earth have you been doing?' said Stefan, still sounding annoyed.

'Goodness, Stefan, that is pretty obvious, I should have thought. Why embarrass them?' drawled Carola.

Angus had flushed scarlet up to the roots of his sandy hair.

'Maggie came as far as the jetty with me to look at the town by moonlight. Is there any law against that?' he asked.

'Well, come along now,' said Stefan, making an obvious effort to control his annoyance. 'We're all going to take the musicians for a midnight barbecue in a valley a few miles away from here.'

They went in the small bus that the Viennese orchestra was using for their travels through Africa and a vast number of people seemed to squeeze themselves in with much laughter and shouting. Angus seemed to have disappeared and somehow Maggie found herself in the back seat of the bus wedged in a corner with Stefan beside her. There was very little room for his broad shoulders and there was nothing else for it but that he should put his arm around her.

After their heated exchange over Angus and her forlorn emotions of the earlier part of the evening, Maggie felt it was somewhat ironical to be in such enforced proximity. The noise of the engine and the crowd was so great that she could not have protested even if she wanted to. But she did not want to. In spite of herself she was happy to be by his side. He had spoken to her as if she was a naughty child and yet all her emotions towards him were those of a woman.

The moon was full casting a soft bright silvery gold light and when they reached the valley where the barbecue was to be held, it looked, with its blue hills receding into the distance, like a landscape upon the moon itself. They all piled out of the bus stretching themselves a little sleepily, but as soon as they were in the bright cool air the company livened up.

Some of the men went off to collect branches of thorn trees and started a fire. Rugs and cushions were produced and put down on the rough stony ground with its frequent thorns, and the company gathered around the fire watching the chops and sausages sizzling on the embers and drinking large tankards of lager and more '*bowle*', but this time it was heated and a burning piece of wood thrust into the liquid before it was put into circulation around the fire.

Carola, Boris and Angus had rejoined Stefan and Maggie and once more Carola engaged Stefan's attention, ignoring the rest. Someone was playing a guitar and the poignant music seemed attuned to Maggie's mood of sadness that was somehow mingled with joy. Stefan, at Carola's persuasion, had wandered away with her to speak to some other friends and Angus had gone to collect some of the cooked meats for the others. Maggie murmured an excuse to Boris and slipped away.

She felt she must get away from the sight of Stefan gaily laughing with Carola. The bright moon made the landscape as clear as day and she followed a goat track until she was at the top of a small hill where there was some kind of old tower. From this point she could see right across the moonlit valley full of strange shadows, in which the bushes and rocks seemed to have a life of their own and to be swaying and moving. She could see many of the queer trees called the Koker Boom standing almost like figures in the distance, with their straight trunks surmounted by a topknot of strangely shaped foliage.

The voices of the people at the party below re-echoed in a queer way amongst the rocks. There was something ghostlike and weird about the strange scenery, and when Maggie heard footsteps coming up the path towards her she was not sure she had heard aright or whether it was the beating of her own heart. But in a moment she recognised the tall form striding effortlessly to where she was standing silhouetted by the silvery light.

'So this is where you are! Really, Maggie, you're more trouble than half a dozen children! I seem to have spent the entire evening looking for you.'

'I hadn't noticed that you particularly desired my company,' Maggie was stung to retort.

'And what do you mean by that? I'm responsible for your safety, aren't I, while you're a guest of ours, and I don't expect you to do senseless things like wandering up a mountain at midnight.'

'It isn't a mountain. It's only a little hill and we're only a few hundred yards away from the rest.'

'Don't argue with me, Maggie. Really, you are the most infuriating child! Don't you know you could have trodden on a night adder or twisted your ankle or any number of things?'

'I'm used to looking after myself,' retorted Maggie sturdily. 'You needn't think you need be a nursemaid to me, Stefan.'

'Nursemaid?' Stefan looked furious. 'I wish I had that much authority with you. For two pins I'd give you a good whipping!'

They glared at each other, their eyes glittering in the silver light.

'I'm not a child,' Maggie declared. 'And I'm not responsible to you for my actions. What right had you to be so rude to Angus at the dance this evening?'

'At the dance? I like that! You chose to absent yourself from the dance with a young man you hardly know and came back entwined in each other's arms for all the world to surmise that you'd been making love together on that romantic jetty.'

'Oh, you...' cried Maggie furiously, and unable to control her anger, slapped him sharply across the face. He laughed out loud and seized both her wrists.

'What a little spitting, scratching tiger kitten! Try fighting someone your own size, Maggie my sweet.'

He let her go and she turned and started to run wildly down to the valley, stumbling over boulders and mounds of anthills.

'Hey, Maggie, silly girl, wait for me!'

She heard his feet pounding behind her and tried to increase her pace, but a loose stone sent her crashing to the ground. For a moment she lay there deprived of breath and then he was bending over her and was sitting on the ground cradling her in his arms.

'Are you hurt? What a foolish little girl you are! For God's sake, why did you have to run away like that?'

He raised her to her feet, disposing of the sandy ground on her dress with a large handkerchief, then gently smoothed her hair back from her face. She looked up at him, her dark eyes enormous in her white face, and suddenly he was kissing her and all the gentleness had gone. He released her so abruptly that she swayed and almost fell once more, but this time he did not come to her aid.

'We must go back to the others,' he said sharply as if the wild embrace had been a figment of her imagination. He took her arm and made her walk quickly down the hillside, making no allowance for her when she stumbled because of his quick pace.

'I must be mad to think I could be in love with such a barbarian,' thought Maggie, shaken and beginning to feel bruised from her fall.

But she knew that when she was alone she would recall the savage passion that he had shown towards her, however briefly, on the wild moonlit hillside.

CHAPTER SEVEN

THEIR return to the party with a rather dishevelled Maggie being helped along by Stefan had not escaped Carola's notice, and she took care that the seating arrangements for the return journey were more to her liking than they had been on the outward one. Maggie was relegated to a seat between Angus and Boris, but in her present state of mind she felt thankful.

She remembered very little of the drive back, for, exhausted with the various experiences of the evening, she fell asleep, only waking when they arrived at their destination to find that she was slumped against Angus's shoulder and that Stefan was regarding them with an angry frown. She closed her eyes to shut out this sight and was aware of their voices above her, though she was too sleepy to take in what they were discussing.

'Poor wee lass, she's dead to the world,' she heard Angus saying. 'How are we to rouse her?'

'Leave her to me,' said Stefan.

At this she stirred a little and protested vaguely, 'I'm almost awake. I can get out of the bus by myself.'

She felt Stefan's strong arms supporting her as he half carried her out of the bus, then as she stood swaying on the pavement he swung her up into his arms and carried her like a child into the house. She opened her eyes and was aware that Carola was standing on the pavement with Boris and was gazing after them with a look of cold disdain.

'Sorry, I didn't mean to be a nuisance,' Maggie murmured as he put her down on the bed.

'That's nothing new, is it?' said Stefan. 'You've been a great nuisance to me all day. You seem to be making a habit of it.'

She glanced at him swiftly, expecting to see that stormy look about his dark grey eyes and craggy features, but he was smiling at her.

'You're such a contrary, exasperating child. I'm sorry I was angry with you this evening, Maggie. Am I forgiven?'

'I suppose so,' said Maggie. It was very difficult to resist him when he was smiling with his face so close to hers and his arms still around her.

'Come then, we'll make up our quarrel in the proper way,' he said, laughing, and before she could stop him he was kissing her once more, but now with a sweet tenderness, as if he were intent on wiping out her memory of that brutal embrace upon the moonlit hillside.

'So sorry, Stefan darling, I didn't realise what I would be interrupting. I came up to see if I could be of any help to Maggie. But I see I'm a little *de trop*.'

It was Carola at the open door, shattering with her cool sophisticated voice the fragile emotion of the moment.

'Oh good, Carola. I'm glad you came. I was going to suggest it.'

Stefan sounded very matter-of-fact and not in the least disconcerted. Maggie reflected that the kiss had been utterly casual and meaningless on his side. Why could she never convince herself in spite of all the evidence that lovemaking was second nature to a man like Stefan?

With a wave of his hand he was gone and she was left alone with a stony-faced Carola, who made not the slightest effort to implement her promise of help, but sat down and looked at Maggie with a gaze of implacable hatred.

Somewhat unnerved by this behaviour, Maggie hastened to assure Carola that she would be all right.

'I don't need any help. All I want to do is to get to bed.'

'You need not think I came to play lady's maid to you,' retorted Carola sharply. 'I did come to help you, but not that way. There is something I think you ought to know.'

Maggie's heart sank. She remembered Matron had once said that if anyone says this it is usually a sign that they want to tell you something unpleasant.

'Don't tell me if it's a secret,' she asked, trying to put off the moment of revelation, for she was sure this was something important.

'It is a secret in a way, but I think you should be told for your own good. You are so young. It doesn't seem fair that you should be treated this way. After all, it is a thing that will affect your whole future.'

Now, of course, Maggie's curiosity was aroused and she would not have stopped Carola if she could.

'My whole future? What is this, Carola?'

'I have decided someone should tell you the reason why Stefan is making up to you.'

'Making up to me?' Maggie was rather astonished. Carola must have noticed the small attentions Stefan had paid to her, Maggie, during the last few days, but in spite of her own feelings, she was sure that to him it did not mean much.

'Oh, for heaven's sake, don't keep repeating everything I say after me like a child at school,' exclaimed Carola ill-temperedly. 'And don't come the innocent on me. I know very well you have been making a play for Stefan, but let me tell you he's not in the least interested in you in spite of appearances. He's only making a fuss of you to please his mother.'

'To please...' Maggie remembered in time Carola's stricture about repetition.

'Let us get down to facts,' said Carola. 'By the terms of his stepfather's will, if Stefan does not marry before or on his thirtieth birthday, which is in a few weeks' time, the castle will revert to Boris's son. Stefan was very wild as a boy and his father was rather straitlaced. Stefan wandered around the world a lot and would not settle down here, so in order to force him to conform his father went as far as changing his will. It was merely to be a gesture. He would have changed it quickly enough if Stefan had come back, but the old man died before this happened.'

'But Stefan loves the castle now,' said Maggie.

'Exactly. And up to now Stefan has shown little in-clination to marry. You will have noticed no doubt he find his pleasures elsewhere. But even to save the castle for her beloved son, the Baroness would never approve of me. Besides, there is no time for us to marry.'

'Why not?' asked Maggie, thoroughly taken aback by Carola's matter-of-fact statement.

'It takes longer than three weeks to get a divorce.' Then seeing Maggie's look of surprise, 'Didn't you know I already had a husband?'

'But I thought ... at least, I heard you had been divorced.'

'Once, yes, but I have since acquired another hus-band, whom I intend to dispense with when I can.

However, the Baroness has cooked up this little plot to marry Stefan to the dear daughter of her beloved friend. It's an old Continental custom, you know, to arrange marriages.'

'You can't mean this,' said Maggie. But even in her bewilderment everything fell into place—the conversation she had overheard, the Baroness's desire to educate her, Boris's hesitancy when she had asked about Sophia's plan, even Stefan ... the thought was like a knife at her heart. Had all Stefan's charm been directed to making her a willing party to this arranged marriage? Had he not even liked her for herself alone, only as a means to an end, the retention of his beloved home?

'You should have heard how Stefan laughed when he told me about it. They were all very taken aback when you arrived. They had expected someone very different.'

'Yes, I realised that,' said Maggie. She closed her eyes, wishing fiercely that Carola would go away now she had made her revelation. She was bruised and aching from her fall, but deep within her there was a much more crushing hurt.

'I'm only telling you this for your own good. It doesn't make much difference to me. Stefan is a wonderful lover, but I have no particular desire to domesticate him as a husband, or to live in that archaic castle with Sophia for a mother-in-law. In fact now I have seen you it might have been a good idea to keep my mouth shut and let them go ahead with the plan.'

It was obvious what Carola meant. She could not regard Maggie as a serious rival, and even if she was Stefan's wife Carola intended to keep a possessive grasp on him still.

'But I feel you are too young to be allowed to go into this with your eyes shut and to be deceived into thinking that Stefan is genuinely interested in you, whereas he and his mother are just using you as a means to an end.'

'What are you suggesting I should do about this?' asked Maggie quietly. She seemed to have gone beyond feeling and was in a state of profound exhaustion.

'Have you your passport with you, and your return ticket?' asked Carola.

'Why, yes.'

'Then it is easy. I will phone Windhoek from the hotel first thing in the morning and make a booking on an outward bound plane for you. Then while the others are busy I can make some excuse and drive you to the airport. No one need know until you have gone. They can hardly bring you back again. They are not your guardians.'

'I must have time to think,' said Maggie. 'Thank you for wanting to help me, Carola, but I'll let you know what I decide first thing in the morning.'

'I will make a provisional booking anyway,' said Carola decisively and, smiling in a more kindly way than she had ever done before, she walked quietly from the room.

When Maggie had showered, she stood beside the window. She was profoundly tired and yet she knew she could not hope to sleep. Why, it was almost morning already! In the cold early light the little town seemed to Maggie to have lost its charm. The whole scene looked depressing and without colour, grey skies, grey sands, grey buildings, grey sea. The cold Atlantic was washing the beaches without breakers and the featureless water made a soft swish, swish, upon the grey white sand.

What was she to do? The clean swift break that Carola had suggested would on the whole be the best. No doubt Sophia would think her ungrateful, but she would get some kind of work on her return to England and scrape and save until she could make some repayment for her air ticket and her clothes. Knowing now about Sophia's intention that she should marry Stefan, she would rather go right away now than have to encounter the persuasive charm of both mother and son.

She knew that in many European countries it was quite usual to arrange marriages of convenience, especially between the children of good friends or colleagues. But feeling about Stefan as she did, how could she face a life with him knowing that he did not truly love her and that, according to Carola, he fully intended to be unfaithful to her?

When later the maid came in with coffee, Maggie had already packed and sorted out the things she intended to take back to England with her. She would leave behind the new clothes she had not worn yet, for they still had the manufacturers' labels on them and perhaps something could be done about returning them.

No one seemed to notice her subdued mood on their journey back to Windhoek, or else everyone else was tired after the late night and they did not think it strange that her hitherto buoyant spirits had disappeared.

Both Boris and Stefan had things to do before they were ready to leave and it was easy enough for Carola and Maggie to slip away without anyone noticing. Carola left her at the barrier of the departure hall and numbly Maggie went through all the formalities of leaving the country. Sitting in the crowded noisy airport, she felt as if she herself was in a pool of silence, separated from the chattering crowds by her own barrier of deep depression. She hardly registered the fact that they had announced that her plane would be late. In any case, what did it matter?

In a few hours she would be back in England and this strange interlude in her life would be over for ever. By accepting Carola's advice she had burned her boats and there could be no turning back. But it was best to make a clean break, however heart-sore she would be in the future.

She remembered Angus's words about Stefan here in this very place. He had said he was ruthless and liked to get his own way and had implied that he trampled roughshod over other people's feelings. Well, she had learned that this was true from bitter experience, for he had played with Maggie's deepest emotions by his careless flirtation and now she knew that he was willing to use her even to the extent of marrying her without love if it served his purpose, which was to secure his beloved castle for himself.

How right Angus had been in his first warning before Maggie had even met Stefan! She should have continued to dislike him as she had at first and never have allowed herself to fall so easily for his careless charm.

They were calling her flight at last when she noticed a commotion going on at the gates. 'You can't do that, sir!' she heard a uniformed official shout, and there, waving him aside, was Stefan leaping the intervening barrier and striding swiftly across towards her. Her heart hammered in her breast as she saw his broad shoulders thrusting their way through the crowd and the tawny head turning this way and that, his grey eyes searching for her. Then he had seen her, and in a few seconds was there where she stood ready to join the queue of waiting passengers. It was as if they were alone for all the notice he took of other people's curious glances. He seized both her arms in his as if he must keep her here by force.

'What's all this, Maggie? Why are you running away? I couldn't believe it when I met Carola and she told me.'

Carola of course could not have realised the plane would be late, or else her pleasure at Maggie's departure had overridden caution.

Maggie gazed tongue-tied at Stefan. How could she tell him why she was leaving?

'Carola said you told her you wanted to go because you were bored and didn't like the country or the people.'

'No, no,' protested Maggie, hurt by his accusing tone. 'It isn't that. I've enjoyed being here.'

Stefan laughed his disbelief.

'So much so that you seize the first opportunity to escape! Obviously you can't stand the idea of going back to the castle. Were you so bored and irritated with our company, then?'

'Oh, Stefan, you know I liked Boris, and your mother I've come to love. I hate to think what her opinion will be, but...'

'But you can't stand me. I might have known.'

'If you want to know,' said Maggie flatly, 'that's partly true. I can't stand your making love to me when it doesn't mean a thing.'

Stefan's brows were frowning, his eyes dark with rage.

'So that's it! At last we get the truth. Just because I kissed you once or twice because you looked sweet and it seemed a pleasant thing to do, now you go rushing off as if I intended to attack your virtue!'

And to Maggie's disgust, with one of his swift changes of mood, he burst out laughing.

She stamped her foot. 'Go on, laugh! Everything is a joke to you. I never met such a hateful man in my whole life. That's why I'm leaving.'

The announcer was shouting the last call for passengers, but Stefan had put his arms around her with a vicelike grip.

'Let me go! I'm catching this plane. You can't stop me now.'

'Oh, can't I? We'll see about that.' He held her close. 'Well, here's another of those so hateful kisses to remember me by,' he said, and kissed her harshly, but she managed to tear herself from his grasp. Now she was running over the tarmac, blinded by tears. She allowed herself one quick backward glance before she entered the plane, but she could see his tall form striding swiftly away. Directed by the stewardess, she sank gratefully into her seat. The girl looked at her with concern.

'Are you feeling well, miss?' she asked. Maggie assured her that she was quite well, then took a mirror from her handbag, curious to know what had occasioned the remark. She did look startlingly pale and dark circles ringed her brown eyes. No wonder the stewardess had commented on this! She fastened her seat belt and closed her eyes wearily as the engines began to warm up. Good. Soon they would be on their way and she could sleep and forget about the last few days.

Her lips felt bruised from Stefan's last fierce kiss, but she must not think about that. The engines were reaching their climax of sound and soon they would be airborne. But a few minutes later the engines seemed to grow quieter and they were still on the ground. She was conscious that someone had stopped in the aisle beside her seat. Two people were talking, one of whom was the stewardess.

'Funny ... I thought she looked pale when I showed her to her seat ... and no wonder!'

A male voice joined in. 'It's a confounded nuisance, but it can't be helped. Better get her off as soon as possible. There's someone waiting who will look after her.'

The stewardess nudged her as she opened her eyes.

'I'm very sorry, miss, we've had word that you're not to be allowed to leave.'

'But my papers are in order. Surely there's nothing to stop me,' stammered Maggie.

'I'm truly sorry, miss, we've had a message from the quarantine people. Our health regulations wouldn't allow you to land. It's far better that you stay here with your friends.'

'But I don't understand.'

The man and the woman both looked at her compassionately.

'Your friend who is waiting for you will explain. Now come, miss, it's no good arguing. I don't suppose you were aware you were breaking regulations. This is all for the best. A good thing we found out before we left. Don't worry about your luggage. We'll have it fumigated and sent back to you after our first stop.'

'Fumigated?' asked Maggie, but they were so busy hustling her off the plane that no one seemed to hear or if they did they did not explain the word. She wanted to bite, scratch, do anything to stay on the plane, but now she was down the steps and the stewardess was helping her firmly and kindly across the runway.

'Goodbye, miss. I hope you go on all right and that this is all a false alarm. Do you realise what you've done to us? We'll all have to have a jab before we're allowed to land.'

The words did not make sense to Maggie and nothing else did either, but the stewardess had gone now, and here was Stefan seizing her by the arm and rushing her towards the waiting car.

'You didn't expect to see me again quite so soon, did you, Maggie darling?'

He was lolling back in the driver's seat, his arm stretched along the back, almost but not quite touching her, a look of complacent self-satisfaction upon his smiling face.

Maggie shook with rage and other conflicting emotions.

'Of course, I knew you had something to do with this, but why did they make me get off the plane?'

'Clever, wasn't it? A sudden brainwave on my part. I knew I had to hijack you off that plane somehow.'

'Well, you're wasting your time and mine too. I intend to sit here until I can get another booking. You can't stop me now. You've delayed me, but I mean to go as soon as I can.'

'Determined little creature, aren't you? But after what I told the health authorities you're going to find it difficult to travel within the next few days.'

Stefan's smug grin infuriated Maggie.

'And what do you mean by that?'

'Only that I said we'd just found out that you'd been in contact with cholera.'

'*What?*'

'It was a lie, of course, but I had to do something to kidnap you off that plane.' He started to laugh. 'Do you realise that all one hundred and fifty people on the plane will have to have anti-cholera injections before they're allowed to land? Already frantic radio messages must be passing between here and London.'

'You're impossible!' declared Maggie. 'Those poor people! I knew you didn't care about anyone else but yourself, but I never thought you could do a thing like this. Why couldn't you let me go?'

But even as she asked, she thought she knew the answer. They were going to try to persuade her to fall in with their plan.

'Don't you know by now that I hate any woman to have a bad opinion of me? We'll start all over again and this time I promise I won't lay one finger upon my easily offended little Maggie.'

He grinned endearingly and put one finger on her lips, then slid his hand under her chin and raised her face to look into his.

'That's a promise,' he said. 'No more kisses until you ask for them.'

'I've still not said I'll go back with you. You take too much for granted. How do you know I won't go to the authorities and tell them how you've lied to them?'

He was still holding her face in his hands and now his expression changed. He looked different now, tender and pleading with all the arrogance vanished.

'If not for mine, I want you to come for my mother's sake. Sophia built so much hope upon your coming. She looked forward to it so much. She doesn't show her feelings easily, but she has become very fond of you in the short time you've been with us.'

Maggie felt her emotions were hopelessly tangled. On the one hand she wanted to believe Stefan. Most of all she wanted to go back to the castle with him and be with him for a little while longer. But what if they were deceiving her...? What if they expected...?

As she hesitated she saw that another car had stopped near at hand and that Boris was coming hastily across the parking lot.

'Stefan, thank heaven I have found you! A message came from the castle half an hour ago to say Sophia is ill. She has had a heart attack. We must return immediately.'

CHAPTER EIGHT

THE medical specialist they had brought with them in Stefan's plane shook his head.

'It would of course be better if we could get her into a hospital, but on the other hand I fear it would be too much for her if we tried to move her. She will need careful nursing. When you take me back I will get a good nurse for you to bring back with you.'

Stefan paced up and down Sophia's sitting-room.

'What could have caused this? She's always seemed to have a constitution of iron.'

The specialist shrugged his shoulders.

'It's difficult to say. She's not getting any younger. She may have had something to worry her lately. Keep her very quiet and rested now. Don't let her get tensed up about anything. She must relax and take things easily.'

'Of course,' agreed Stefan. He turned to Maggie. 'I'll be back as soon as I can make it, bringing a nurse, I hope. Meanwhile do you think you'll be able to cope with things here?'

All Maggie's anger at his high-handed ways had vanished in a great desire to be of help and to wipe away the expression of tragic dread from his face.

'Try not to worry, Stefan. I'm quite experienced in caring for sick people. I promise I'll do my best.'

Stefan did not look very reassured.

'You're so young to leave alone with all this responsibility. But it won't be for long, I promise. It may be too dark to return this evening, but I'll return at first light. Ask Boris and Serafina for anything you need. I know Boris will be of help, though naturally he's not very practical about domestic things.'

Maggie thought that the same thing could probably be said about Stefan, but she held her tongue. She wanted to kiss away the worried look from his face and again see his eyes light up with mischievous laughter, but he was withdrawn and cold, and she remembered his promise at the airport. There would be no more flirtatious kisses.

Sophia's bedroom was the largest one in the castle, beautiful with faded Aubusson carpets in blue, rose and cream and with a great gilded bed with painted headboard. Sophia, looking very fragile, sat propped against lacy pillows. She held her hand out to Maggie and grasped it firmly.

'It is good to see you again, Marguerite. I have been lying here thinking about your mother and thinking about you too. How happy she would have been if she could have known that our two children would make friends and travel together!'

Maggie breathed a prayer of thankfulness that she had been prevented from going home. It would have been dreadful if the others had had to tell Sophia that she had gone away. Almost immediately Sophia sank into a deep sleep as the result of the injections she had had, and Maggie went in search of Serafina to sit with her mistress, while she, Maggie, unpacked and washed after the hurried journey. She found her in the small ante-room near Sophia's bedroom. Her usually imperturbable, dignified demeanour was disturbed by her anxious expression.

'How did the doctor say my madam is?' she asked Maggie.

'He said she's not well and must rest quietly,' Maggie informed her.

'It was the phone call,' said Serafina, shaking her head. 'My madam was well until the phone call came.'

'Who phoned her?' asked Maggie.

It seemed unlikely that any kind of phone call would disturb the calm dignity of Stefan's mother.

'I do not know. But it was after she had been talking that she called me and could not get her breath.'

It must have been a coincidence, thought Maggie. Nothing had been said about a phone call. Sophia herself had not told them anything had happened. But then she seemed a little dazed.

Sophia's room looked out on to the Garden of Love, and Maggie sat there in the late afternoon having given Serafina instructions to call her if the Baroness awoke. The temporary confiscation of her suitcase had resulted in her being left with all the new clothes she had left behind and, thinking to please Sophia, she had put on one of her prettiest dresses, a thin voile in turquoise colour with very dainty cuffs of white cambric and broderie anglaise edging.

She was sitting at the edge of the pool, idly watching the goldfish flick hither and there amongst the green water weeds, when she was suddenly aware that she was being watched. She looked up with a start of surprise into the eyes of a total stranger, a man who was tall, slimmer than Stefan, and with dark, still eyes and hair glossy as the pelt of a black panther.

'Don't get up,' he said. 'No one was around, so I let myself in. I phoned the Baroness to let her know I was coming.'

'She didn't tell me,' said Maggie, confused. 'At least ... there hasn't been time, because she's ill.'

'Ill? But I spoke to her this morning. She seemed perfectly well then. In fact she had some rather harsh things to say to me, but no matter. I'm sorry, I should have introduced myself. I am Alexis von Linsingen. Doubtless you know my father, who lives here. Are you a house guest?'

So this was Boris's son. Now the riddle of Sophia's sudden heart attack seemed solved. If Alexis had phoned and said something to worry her, this could have caused it. But then Maggie reflected that she had no right to think this and that she was prejudiced because he was to take Stefan's place in the castle if ... But all this was only surmise. All the same, she did not like this man on first acquaintance. She felt a small frisson of fear as he stood regarding her shrewdly with his still dark eyes in the thin saturnine face.

Maggie introduced herself. It appeared that Alexis had come here by road and had phoned Sophia during the journey.

'Dear Sophia! She was quite surprised to hear from me. I've been wandering around Europe during the last few years.'

'I suppose you would like to see your father now,' said Maggie, anxious to get rid of his company and go back to the Baroness.

'No hurry. It's much pleasanter to sit in this beautiful garden with a pretty young girl than to meet a father who invariably disapproves of one's behaviour.'

'I'm afraid I'll have to go to Sophia. I'll call a maid to show you to your room. There are always rooms prepared for guests here.'

'But I too wish to see Sophia as soon as possible.'

His mouth smiled in a lazy cynical fashion, but the expression did not reach those dark eyes.

'I'm afraid that won't be possible,' said Maggie firmly. 'The doctor said she was to have no visitors at all.'

'But I'm not a visitor. I'm a close relative. Surely you must realise that. Oh, I suppose you're worried because I said she spoke to me sharply. It was only my little joke, my dear Marguerite. She was just making some rather brisk remarks comparing me to a prodigal son. I assure you that she'll be very glad to see me. In fact she begged me to get here as soon as possible so that we could discuss family affairs.'

Maggie wished desperately that Stefan was here. He would have made short work of Alexis's intention to see Sophia. If she went to consult Boris, Alexis might take the opportunity to go to Sophia's room. What was she to do?

All that she could hope for was that he would not dare to upset Sophia if she herself were there. She went up the staircase towards the bedroom wondering how she could put him off.

'I rather think she'll be sleeping,' she said. 'The doctor said she must have as much rest as possible.'

'Let us go and see first, little Marguerite. I assure you she'll be pleased to see me.'

And he followed her along the corridor like the dark ghost of one of the family portraits that hung upon the wall. But at the antechamber of Sophia's room he received a check. Giselle and Sacha were sitting like two images of dogs on either side of the door. They allowed Maggie to pass through unhindered, but when Alexis tried to follow, they sprang towards him with low growls.

When Maggie spoke to them they desisted, but, each time he tried to pass, the threatening thunder started once more from their throats. Maggie was very relieved that the matter had been taken out of her hands in such an unexpected way. It was plain that whatever happened the silvery white Russian hunting dogs would not allow Alexis to visit their beloved mistress.

'This is ridiculous! They should be tied up,' Alexis said angrily.

'Perhaps they can be tied later,' Maggie promised, not very sincerely, and she sent Serafina to show Alexis to his room.

Sophia had awakened and was puzzled by the noise of the dogs.

'Is there a stranger here?' she asked.

'No, the dogs were barking because they were pleased to see me, I think,' Maggie fibbed.

Sophia did not look satisfied with this explanation, but said nothing more. She lay for a while tracing the pattern of the silken coverlet with her long slender hand.

'Tell me, Marguerite,' she asked finally, 'have you any romantic interest in England yet? I mean any boyfriend who attracts you?'

Maggie shook her head. 'I've hardly had time to form any attachment of that nature because I've always been at school and living in the orphanage up to now, you know.'

'Yes, I suppose so. You will think it a little foolish, my dear, but I have been lying here thinking how your mother and I used to talk together. In those days before the war we were rather romantically minded and we used to plan that if ever we had a son and a daughter, maybe some day they would please us both by marrying each other.'

Maggie wanted to turn the Baroness away from the

subject and so she said briskly, 'And now that you've met me, I suppose you think that idea was a little foolish.'

'By no means,' said the Baroness, and took Maggie's hand. 'Perhaps at first I must admit I had been expecting some kind of replica of your dear mother, but now I have got to know you better I have come to like you, my dear, very much indeed.'

'Please don't go on,' begged Maggie. 'I like you very much too, but the other idea is impossible. You must see that. I could never marry without love.'

Sophia sighed and let her hand fall from Maggie's grasp.

'So you have not succumbed to my Stefan's charm. What a pity! I would like you for a daughter, my dear.'

It was best, thought Maggie, that Sophia should think that she did not like Stefan. Otherwise her position would be intolerable. But Sophia did not give up easily.

'You know,' she said, 'these arranged marriages often turn out to be very happy ones. We European people are not as sentimental as people who have been brought up in the English tradition of marriage for love. My own first marriage was arranged and I was perfectly happy, not perhaps as happy as when I married my second husband, but then the circumstances were very different.'

'Please don't talk about it any more,' begged Maggie. 'You're tiring yourself with all this conversation. You must rest.'

Dinner that evening was a rather uncomfortable affair. Maggie would have liked to have had hers in her room, but did not want to cause any more inconvenience to the household. It was obvious that Boris was taken aback and not too pleased by his son's arrival. He was still charming to Maggie, but in an abstracted way, and the conversation between himself and Alexis was awkward and double-edged.

Alexis had helped himself very freely to whisky before dinner and proceeded to drink the wine that was always at hand in Continental custom. As the evening wore on he became openly quarrelsome and aggressive with his father.

'My dear Father,' he expostulated, 'can you give me one good reason why I should not be allowed to greet Tante Sophia? Surely a visit from a relative, whom she has not seen for a long time, would do her good, knowing her family feeling?'

'Have some common sense, for heaven's sake, Alexis. Sophia must be kept quiet. It will do her no good to have a visit from you.'

'Really? Now that's interesting. But I suppose everyone else connected with the household can come and go freely. Why should her room be forbidden to me? I'm quite sure she would be shocked if she knew a dear relative was being kept at bay by guard dogs.'

'You exaggerate as usual, Alexis. But I must beg you not to disturb her or anyone else here, especially since you came uninvited.'

'Since when has a son needed an invitation to visit his father?'

Boris sighed. The eyes of Alexis were becoming bloodshot, his speech slurred. He was drinking a generous helping of brandy with his coffee, and Maggie wondered if she could leave him to Boris now and slip up to Sophia.

She murmured some excuse and stole away, worried

134

by the loud voice echoing up the stairs. However, Sophia's bedroom was away from the main wing. She could hardly hear him unless they went out into the garden. When she entered the room, Sophia was asleep with Serafina sitting by her side. There was nothing more she could do here. Asking the maid to call her if she needed her, she went to her room, glad to retire after the eventful happenings of the day.

Her own kimono had disappeared in the London-bound plane and by this time must be in London Airport. But amongst her purchases was a more sophisticated gown of a deep peacock blue. It flowed to her feet and gave to her small figure an unaccustomed air of dignity. She sat for a while on the little balcony outside her window looking over the distant desert. Far away the clouds were indigo and blue-grey colour, and every now and again there were vivid bursts of savage lightning and the distant roll of thunder. Soon they had told her the rain might come to relieve the heat.

She thought of Stefan again spending the night in Windhoek. Was he with Carola? Carola would be pleased that she did not have to share him this time. She wondered how Carola, even if she had been married twice before, could say that she was not considering marriage to Stefan. If one loved a man surely one wanted to spend a lifetime with him, not merely have an affair? And if Stefan truly loved someone, she could not imagine that he would be satisfied with anything less than marriage. It was all rather puzzling. She hoped Sophia would recover soon and then she herself could go back to England and her normal life, far away from Stefan's magnetic presence.

There was a soft knock at the door and thinking it was Serafina come to give her news of Sophia she called

'Come in!' but her worry was turned to alarm as she saw Alexis sidling in with a sly smile on his dark face. She started up exclaiming, 'Is anything wrong? What...?'

'Nothing, my dear child, nothing at all. Don't alarm yourself, Marguerite. This is just a sociable visit.'

His speech was slurred and it was obvious that he had been partaking pretty freely of the fine claret that Boris usually served after dinner for himself and Stefan.

'It's a long time since I've dined and wined so well,' he said, lurching further into the room. 'I really must come to visit my revered parent more often.'

'I'm glad you enjoyed it,' Maggie replied, trying to be tactful. Whatever she did, she thought, she must try not to annoy him. He looked as if he could be a very difficult man if crossed. 'But, Alexis, you must have had a very long day, and I'm rather tired too. Don't you think it might be a good idea if you got some sleep now?'

Alexis waved this aside.

'Plenty of time, my dear Marguerite. The night is young. You don't think I'm going to pass up the opportunity to make the acquaintance of an attractive young girl? It's not often Sophia has one staying in the castle. Too careful of her dear son, I dare say. But coming to think of it, that isn't strictly correct. Lately she's been all eagerness to get her Stefan married off before his thirtieth birthday. You know of this condition, of course? That's why you've come, I dare say.'

Maggie stepped back as if he had slapped her.

'I knew nothing of these conditions when I came here, Alexis, and I'm not in the least interested now.'

'No? Then you're a girl after my own heart. You're

on my side?'

'Certainly not. I'm on no one's side, as you call it.'

But Alexis was engrossed in his own rather muddled thoughts.

'Not interested in the fascinating Stefan, eh? That's unusual. But all the better for me.' He laughed in a rather satirical way and sat down rather unsteadily upon the bed, patting a place beside him and saying, 'Come over here, Margarita. Don't be so unfriendly.'

'You must excuse me, Alexis. I'll see you tomorrow. I really don't feel very sociable tonight. It's been a long day.'

He laughed, and at the same time stretched out one hand and seized the long skirt of her gown, so that she had to draw nearer or risk standing before this intoxicated man in a flimsy nightgown. But before she could realise what he intended, he had ripped open the front of the peacock gown and clasped her in his arms, his hot hands bruising her tender skin.

'What's wrong?' he demanded, as she struggled. 'If you're not engaged to Stefan, what's wrong with a little friendly lovemaking? You needn't be afraid anyone will know. We're too far away for any of the household to hear.'

It was true. Stefan was away, Sophia ill with Serafina in attendance and Boris probably cooped up in his workshop. She would have to cope with this situation on her own. He had drawn her down towards him and was pressing his hot face against her body so that she could feel his lips through the thin material of her gown.

'You have no right to come to my room,' she said indignantly, 'especially in this state. Let me go, Alexis! If any harm comes to me while I'm here with Sophia,

Stefan will see to it that you get what you deserve.'

'Stefan is far away and no one can hear us. Why be so shy, Marguerite? You haven't had such a sheltered upbringing. Surely a girl from London must have been around? Every girl dreams of experiencing romance, and I could teach you so much.'

He was pressing her backwards upon the bed, holding her down with a brutal grip. She felt herself half fainting, her strength almost gone. But he had left the door slightly open, so convinced was he that they would not be disturbed, and now there was a flash of white.

Giselle came bounding through, pushing the heavy door with the savage strength of all her hunting ancestors. In seconds she was upon Alexis, attacking him with swift cruel nips of her sharp teeth. Ignominiously he ceased his unwelcome attentions and turned on his heels with Giselle pursuing him down the corridor baying deeply until Maggie called her back into the room and locked the door.

'Oh, Giselle, you were wonderful!' Maggie assured the beautiful animal, caressing her silky silver head. 'What would I have done without you?' Giselle settled down upon her favourite fur rug, giving small warning growls as if to threaten all intruders.

In spite of her agitation, Maggie slept soundly undisturbed for the rest of the night, but woke at early dawn just as the morning star was showing itself at her window and the first light was coming. She wondered if Stefan was on his way back. She hoped so much that he would come soon. It was far too difficult being alone in the castle with a character like Alexis.

And yet she hesitated to complain about his behaviour to Boris. But she was determined that she must keep him from visiting Sophia. As for herself, how would he behave towards her after his setback last night? His feelings towards her could hardly be very kindly.

She dressed hurriedly, meaning to go to Sophia's room to relieve Serafina, but the Herero woman came in to her with a tray of coffee and croissants, and assured her that Sophia was sleeping after spending a good night. She had left a younger maid with the Baroness while she attended to her household duties, but Maggie tried to be as quick as possible over her light breakfast so that she could return to Sophia.

She was not feeling worried about Alexis as she felt sure he must be sleeping off his indulgences of the previous night, but in that, she was to learn later, she was mistaken. As she went downstairs to let out Giselle into the sparkling sunlit morning, Samgau the little Bushman came towards her.

'Master will be back soon,' he assured her.

'How do you know, Samgau?' asked Maggie. 'I've heard no plane.'

'I feel it here,' said the little man, pointing to his chest.

Stefan had told her that Bushmen seemed to have a kind of sixth sense and to be able to tell when people were coming long before they did. Sure enough, a while afterwards as Maggie was proceeding to Sophia's room, she heard the plane overhead.

As she entered the sitting-room leading to Sophia's bedroom, she was puzzled to hear voices in the inner room. Was Sophia talking to the maid? But it sounded louder than the soft African voice of the domestics. She walked forward, her footsteps muffled by the thick carpet. Alexis was sitting at the foot of Sophia's bed, leaning forward and gesticulating to emphasise a point in his conversation.

'My dear Sophia, you must admit if you think about things sensibly that you should resign yourself to the fact that I will inherit the castle, not Stefan. Why are you unwilling to talk about it? If you treat me politely I might even be willing to retain Stefan as manager. But I would insist on living here myself, of course. You and Stefan could live in the foreman's house. It's quite adequate, I understand.'

The Baroness was sitting erect upon her pillow. She looked white and fragile, dark circles encircling her eyes, and it was obviously a great effort to maintain her dignified poise.

'Stefan is not yet thirty,' she breathed. 'Until that day, I would be glad, Alexis, if you would keep clear of this place. Your own father forbade you to come again the last time you paid us a visit.'

'Stefan had better hurry if he's to retain the castle,' blustered Alexis, a little taken aback by the sick woman's proud response. 'Who are you proposing he should marry? The little girl from overseas? You seem to have backed a loser there, Sophia. She told me herself she's not interested in your charming son.'

'Marguerite? She has been talking to you? She has confided in you?'

This was more than Maggie could stand, and she came into the room.

'Good morning, Sophia. How are you this morning? Alexis, I would be glad if you could leave now. I have to attend to the Baroness.'

Alexis rose from his seat at the foot of the bed.

'Think it over, my dear Sophia. You'll have to consent eventually to my plans for running the castle.

There's no other way.'

With a malignant glance at Maggie, he strode out of the room.

Maggie was alarmed by Sophia's pallor.

'Would you like one of your tablets?' she asked, but the Baroness waved her aside.

'I did not think it of you that you would discuss my son with that wretched creature,' she whispered. 'But of course I can hardly blame you, for you do not know the circumstances. Nevertheless, Marguerite, I should have thought you would be able to sense what a loathsome person he is, even if he does happen to be poor Boris's son.'

'Try not to agitate yourself, Sophia dear,' implored Maggie, not wanting to argue with the sick woman. 'I dislike Alexis as much as you seem to do. Don't think about him. I've just heard Stefan's plane. He should be here at any moment now.'

'Stefan? Oh, my dear, leave me and go to meet him. Bring him straight here. I must see him at once to tell him about Alexis.'

As Maggie paused on the great staircase above the musicians' gallery, she saw the huge door burst open. Stefan stood looking up at her, but his greeting was drowned by the joyous barking of Sacha and Giselle. She hurried down, wanting to reassure him immediately about his mother's condition, and even as she approached him she remembered with regret that before the scene at the airport he would have caught her in his arms and greeted her affectionately, but he had promised, and she knew he was a man of his word that he 'would not lay one finger on "my easily offended Maggie"'.

He frowned when she told him the news of the

arrival of Alexis. 'It could hardly have come at a worse time,' he said. 'But I trust you kept him from my mother.'

'I tried, Stefan. The whole of yesterday, I kept him away, but this morning...'

Stefan frowned, his eyes like stormy grey cloud.

'This morning?'

'He managed to get in to visit her. Stefan, I'm afraid it harmed her.'

'Heavens, Maggie, surely you could have prevented it. Why did I leave her in the care of a child!'

He ran up the stairs two at a time with the two dogs close behind him. Maggie stood as if he had struck her, then ascended more slowly. She could hear him calling her as she reached the passage leading to Sophia's room.

'Good grief, Maggie, come quickly! She's had another attack!'

CHAPTER NINE

THE heart specialist had come and gone in the plane that Stefan had chartered from Windhoek, but he had left a nurse with instructions for Sophia's treatment, a large efficient Afrikaans lady called Mrs. du Toit. If Alexis tried any more importunities he would get short shrift at her hands. The worst seemed to be over for the time being, but Sophia was still very ill.

This was what Stefan was telling Maggie as they sat in the tower room. It was the place, Maggie recalled, where he had given her that first gay, passionate kiss. But now the light and laughter had gone from his expression.

'The specialist assured me Maman has a very short time to live. I've explained the terms of my father's will to you, and now I'm asking you, Maggie, begging you to marry me so that Maman can die in peace. She'll be satisfied if she knows I'll inherit the castle. And afterwards you'll be free to go. I don't delude myself for a moment that you wish to stay after your attempt at flight that other time.'

'But, Stefan, this marriage ... it wouldn't mean anything, then?'

She longed for just one word of tenderness, but he mistook her meaning. She turned her face away to escape from the frowning distress in his.

'The marriage will be a technicality only. When all this is over, you may choose any kind of training you desire. But I wouldn't insult you, Maggie, by offering you a bribe. I'm throwing myself on your mercy. My main concern is for my mother, not for myself, whatever you may think of me.'

Strangely enough Maggie was prepared to believe this. She knew he loved the castle and the life here very much, but she could imagine that for himself he could settle somewhere else and make a new life. But he did not want his mother's last days to be disturbed by the grinding worry of seeing the hated Alexis taking his place, nor did he want to see her turned out of her home at the end of her life.

Maggie looked at Stefan. Was it not partly her fault that Sophia had suffered another attack? She longed to take the large brown hands in hers and to kiss away the frown below the tawny rough curls. Her heart quailed at the idea that he had presented to her, that they should marry and it should be 'a technicality only', and that later when Sophia had gone, for the specialist had warned that her life could be numbered in weeks only, she should go back to England and take up training for a career as if nothing had happened.

But her love for Stefan, together with the affection that had grown for Sophia, would not let her abandon them to Alexis and his plans if she could help it.

'Very well, Stefan,' she said solemnly. 'You can tell Sophia I've consented to marry you.'

For a moment the old gay expression flickered across Stefan's rugged face. He made a move towards her and her heart beat wildly as she thought he was going to take her in his arms, but his hands fell to his sides.

'I won't forget the promise I made when you came back, Maggie. You're an angel. I swear you won't regret this.'

It was almost worth her heartache to see Sophia's joy

144

when they broke the news to her. She gestured to Stefan that he should open the wall safe that was concealed behind a picture in her room. From an old rosewood box lined with quilted red satin she produced a very beautiful square cut emerald ring.

'Your hand is slender and small, like mine, Marguerite,' she whispered. 'This should fit. Let me see you put it on her, Stefan.'

He slipped the heavy gold ring upon her left hand.

'Pledge it with a kiss,' Sophia whispered faintly, and Maggie felt Stefan's cold firm lips kissing her in a gesture that she was convinced meant nothing.

During the next few days Sophia, with her indomitable spirit, rallied amazingly.

'It would be appropriate,' she said, one day when Maggie was sitting beside her, 'if you could be married on Stefan's thirtieth birthday. You realise, of course, that it is essential to marry on that day or before. It would give me time to recover my health a little if there was some intervening time. I am afraid we will not be able to obtain much trousseau for you, Marguerite, but that can be remedied later.'

'You've given me enough already,' Maggie assured her.

She was deeply alarmed at the sudden realisation that she was actually going to have to fulfil her promise. Already Sophia had ordered the wedding invitations and was organising arrangements for the reception. In spite of the fact that Stefan pleaded with her that they should be married very quietly, the Baroness was determined to have some guests. She asked Stefan to arrange to have the Viennese orchestra come to the castle for two days and Serafina was instructed to hire extra servants from amongst her relatives. She asked

Maggie to look in one of the ancient wardrobes to find a most beautiful cream satin wedding gown which had been Sophia's own, together with a veil of exquisite lace that had been worn by the brides of her family for generations.

She had also ordered that hundreds of pink roses should be flown from Johannesburg on the day before the wedding, and now she had another fancy.

'My dear Boris, would you be able to make a unicorn from rose quartz?'

'Of course, darling Sophia. How big would you want it?'

'Not very big, Boris, but I would need one as a gift for each guest.'

Boris looked a little taken aback at the magnitude of her request, but he would not have denied them to her if she had asked for a thousand.

'I will have to organise an expedition to the mountains to find sufficient quantity,' was all he said.

'Near the mine where you can buy rose quartz there are Bushman paintings, aren't there?' asked Sophia. 'It would be a good idea if you could take Maggie there. She has hardly stirred out of the castle since I have been ill. Stefan could take you in the plane as far as possible and you could do it in one day.'

Finally it was decided that they should organise an expedition including Stefan, Boris and Maggie and taking Samgau along with them as a guide. Boris decided he would phone Angus and ask if he could come for the weekend and join in the expedition because his knowledge of rocks always came in useful. Maggie had hoped Alexis would not get to hear of the proposed trip, but of course it was too difficult to keep it from him. However, they were most relieved when he announced that he was going to visit farming friends for the weekend.

Maggie had been a little worried when she thought of leaving Sophia alone in the castle with Alexis. The nurse would be there, of course, but she felt much happier when she understood that Alexis would be away.

It had been arranged that Angus should arrive in his station wagon the night before the expedition was to take place, and as she dressed for dinner Maggie was happy to hear the sound of a vehicle arriving. It would be good to see Angus again. He gave a touch of practicality and common sense to her present romantic surroundings. Angus would not have been flattered if he had known, but in Maggie's estimation he seemed to fill the gap she felt by the loss of Matron's companionship.

The plain white crêpe dress displayed the perfect beauty of her ring and the matching emerald brooch that Sophia had insisted she should accept. When she had taken it the thought had crossed her mind that it was on loan only. When she returned to England, the ring and brooch would stay here. This jewellery, the first that Maggie had ever possessed, looked very precious to her, even more so because Stefan had placed the ring on her finger and pinned the brooch upon her dress.

On the way down to dinner she called in to see Sophia. Propped up against the lacy pillows, Sophia still looked very frail, but there was a brilliance in her eyes that belied this. It was plain that as long as she could she would cling on to life, certainly during the time that must elapse before Stefan and Maggie married.

'Are you sure you want us to leave you tomorrow?'

Maggie asked. 'Will you be all right?'

'Certainly,' asserted Sophia, her voice quite strong and determined. 'I am very much better now and I am very keen that you should see a bit more of this wonderful country. I am sure you will be most intrigued with the Bushman paintings. Besides, I have set my heart on Boris getting the rose quartz to make the unicorns.'

Maggie spoke to Nurse du Toit in the anteroom.

'She's much better,' this rotund homely body assured her. 'How long it can last, goodness knows, but at this time she seems to be enjoying some remission of her symptoms. She'll be quite all right with me. You need have no fears about that.'

Somewhat reassured by this, Maggie made her way back along the corridor on her way down to the hall, but rounding the bend of the graceful curved staircase, she paused, astonished by a familiar sound. There was no mistaking that alluring laugh. Carola! What was she doing here? The huge stone fireplace made a striking background for her fabulous hair and the generous curves of her willowy figure in its clinging dress that was the colour of flame.

'Surprise, surprise!' she exclaimed as Maggie came down the stairs. 'I met Angus in town and asked him where he was going to with all his equipment, and when I found out he was coming to the castle, naturally I knew you would all be delighted if I joined in the party.'

Angus looked a little abashed, but Maggie could understand that it would have been very difficult for a man of his nature to withstand Carola's skilled persuasion.

'And I understand we must congratulate you, Maggie, though of course it isn't done to congratulate the future bride, is it? But in this case . . .' She let her voice trail away. 'Stefan told me you had decided it would be better to stay. Oh well, Maggie, one doesn't get the chance to marry a castle every day, does one? Any girl of your upbringing would seize the chance to be a beggar maid to King Cophetua, I suppose, regardless of how the king really thought of her.'

This last was uttered in a low voice so that only Maggie could hear. She really does hate me, thought Maggie, in spite of her coolness when she told me she did not want to marry Stefan. In all her life Maggie had never felt herself hated. It was an odd, rather terrifying sensation. She turned aside and encountered another malignant gaze, that of Alexis. It was a relief to make conversation with Angus and to make his rather dour expression change to appreciative laughter. Stefan, who had been helping Boris to pour the aperitifs, glanced frowning towards them, but she hardly noticed. She was so anxious to blot out the memory of Carola's waspish comments and of the brooding saturnine frowns of Alexis.

After dinner Carola persuaded Stefan to play some Spanish and South American music on his record player. The throbbing exotic sound disturbed Maggie, and when Stefan started dancing with Carola to the slow sensuous strains that changed in a few moments to passionate fiery rhythm she felt she could not endure it. Yet what right had she to object to Carola's flaunting attachment to Stefan? Her coming marriage was an arranged thing, a matter of convenience only. Regarding Stefan's whipcord strength as he gave himself to the passion of the dance and whirled Carola around until her hair spun in a silver cloud, she thought she must have been mad to consent to their scheme.

Boris drew her aside to ask if she would join him in showing the castle to Angus and she was glad to get away from the romantic scene. They finished their tour in Boris's workshop where she made coffee for the two men.

When she and Angus came back to the hall, the dancing had stopped. Carola's white hands were entwined closely around Stefan's broad shoulders and his head bent very close to hers. He broke away from this intimate attitude when he saw the other pair and Carola gave a small silvery trill of laughter.

'So sorry, Maggie. Habits are hard to break, aren't they, Stefan?'

Stefan frowned and looked displeased, but whether it was because of her remark or because they had been interrupted in a near-embrace, Maggie did not know. She was enlightened, however, when she met him alone in the corridor leading to his mother's suite. She had discovered that Sophia was sleeping and so had turned to go back without entering the bedroom when she was rather startled to see his tall form looming up in the subdued light of the passage.

'I would like a word with you, Maggie, but not here. Come to the tower room.'

What now? she thought, and followed him silently to the tower. When they arrived he seemed to hesitate, pacing up and down the narrow confines of the room for all the world like an angry lion in a cage. Finally he halted in front of her where she sat straight up and unrelaxed in one of the red leather chairs.

'Maggie, I fully realise that you're doing me a favour

by consenting to go through with this marriage, so that in itself puts me in an awkward position.'

'In what way do you mean, Stefan?' Maggie thought for a moment that on seeing Carola again he had decided he could not go through with it.

'I mean you may feel you have every right to resent criticism, but you're young and inexperienced and I feel I must tell you that while this engagement and so-called marriage are operative I must demand from you the same standard of conduct as I would demand of a true bride.'

Maggie was on her guard. 'In what way have I offended you, Stefan?'

'Surely you must realise that it's hardly seemly for you to show you're so pleased to see Angus and to spend the evening in his company?'

Maggie felt as if she could actually feel a flame of anger flicker through her like lightning striking a young tree.

'That really is one of the funniest things I've heard for a long time! How dare you accuse me of being interested in Angus? Why, you've spent the whole evening making up to Carola!'

'I can hardly be rude to a guest in my house.'

'You seemed to be stretching politeness to the limit when we came back into the hall and saw you together. A guest ... and an uninvited one at that!'

To her surprise Stefan smiled with that wicked grin that attracted her too much while at the same time it made her furiously angry.

'Why, little Maggie, I do believe you're jealous!'

She felt she would have liked to hit that teasing smile from off the rugged face with its dark grey eyes watching her every expression.

'Oh, how I hate you when you say stupid things to me like that! If it wasn't that I've given my word to Sophia I would be on the first plane tomorrow. And I wouldn't care if I never saw you again!'

'I know well enough how you feel about me. But we must go through with this farce now we've pledged our word. Don't worry, Maggie, I certainly won't take advantage of your position, and you can leave as soon as you wish to after...'

He was silent and again she experienced the swift reversal of feelings that she seemed to have whenever she was with him. Tenderness and pity replaced her former anger, but there was no way to show him this.

'We have to make an early start tomorrow, I know,' she said stiffly. 'Will you excuse me now, Stefan?'

'Certainly.'

His expression was cold and distant as he opened the door, but as she descended the stairs, she was conscious that he still stood there, looking after her.

It was barely light when their plane descended to the airstrip nearest to the mountainous area where they were to obtain the rose quartz, and by the time the sun rose they were well on their way in the four-wheel-drive vehicle provided for their use. As they drove across a plain, the distant range of hills gradually came into view with rounded mountains looking rather like a group of crouching lions. Covered at first with grey mists, now they were coloured with shimmering crimson that became lighter as the sun rose higher until the scene was ablaze with flaming light.

Near at hand the whole landscape was shimmering in the rising sun, the thin grass turning from silver to gold as it was caught by the cool breeze of morning, while the small gnarled thorn trees stood out in black silhouette. Maggie spied a movement to her left.

'What's that?' she called excitedly.

'A herd of zebras and wildebeeste, Samgau says. The farmers in this neighbourhood are keen on preserving the wild life. Here are my glasses. You'll be able to see more clearly with them.'

Stefan stopped the vehicle and Maggie gazed through the binoculars at the fat striped zebras and the wildebeeste with their queer top-heavy heads and narrow hindquarters. Then she saw a herd of springboks with shining coats of tan and white and neat curved horns, leaping high into the air as if in sheer joy of living on this wonderful morning.

As she moved the glasses around, she thought she could see a puff of dust from another vehicle far away in the direction from which they had come. She was just going to comment on this to Stefan when Carola gave an exclamation of impatience and said, 'Really, Maggie, haven't you seen enough? We can't stand here all day.'

So she handed the glasses back to Stefan without remarking upon the fact that she had seen the dust. In any case it was probably just a small whirlwind in the distance, for it was unusual to see any other travellers in this vast landscape.

Boris had arranged that the farmer upon whose land the quartz quarry was should meet them with a train of mules at the point where the path became impossible to negotiate by motor vehicle.

The plain itself over which they had come had been made of stony ground with only a light covering of grass, but now at the bottom of the hills the rocks became more numerous, larger and very queer-shaped. Soon they came close together to form a kind of gorge.

On the plain the sun as soon as it had risen had blazed down with a fierce burning heat mitigated only slightly by the breeze, but within the gorge they were suddenly plunged into cold shaded gloom.

Mr. Macpherson, the farmer, led the way followed by Stefan with Samgau running by his side. He was followed by Carola who had carefully placed herself between Boris and Stefan so that Maggie was forced to the back with Angus following. It seemed that this track must once have been a river bed, but now it was dry and sandy with the characteristic '*blinkhaar*' or 'shining hair' grass growing up between the stones and with a few acacia thorn bushes struggling towards the light.

'It's so very gloomy and without life,' whispered Maggie to Angus. There was something about the dark gorge that made you feel you had to speak quietly.

'Yes, it's no the most cheerful place you could find,' Angus agreed. 'But it improves later on.'

Maggie had said it was lifeless, and indeed it seemed so after the plains with their pretty pronking springboks, but now she saw some large birds wheeling in flight above the gorge, their huge black and white wings motionless in the still blue air.

'What are those birds?' she asked.

'Those? Those are vultures,' Angus answered.

Maggie shuddered, although at this distance they looked harmless enough. Except for the fact that one felt less closed in, when they emerged from the narrow gorge, Maggie found that the scene was just as terrifying. Huge granite boulders lay around and the bulging queer-shaped masses of bare rock gave the appearance of something not quite of this world. Everywhere great pieces of rock lay around as if they had been torn away

154

by giants engaged in some primeval battle.

It was all so closed in that the sharp morning light had not yet penetrated to the bottom of the mountain, but above the blue slopes were turning to pinkish gold in the warm sunlight. She shook off her queer stupid sense of foreboding and heard them discussing the fact that this was where Stefan, Carola and herself were going to ascend the hills to look for Bushman paintings. The farmer was to take Boris and Angus with Samgau to get the rose quartz and they would join the others later.

Maggie's mule was slow because Boris had tried to pick out the quietest one for her. It lingered upon the track and she saw with dismay that Carola was urging her mount quickly forward as if deliberately trying to separate herself and Stefan. He kept glancing back and urging her to go a bit faster. But time and again she found herself alone on the track in this rather frightening wilderness of stone sloping upwards to the great rampart of rock on the summit.

On one of these occasions she was aware in the still morning air of the sound of hoofs on the rock. Of course it must be from the mules in front of her. But she could have sworn it came from behind as if someone was riding parallel with her but on a higher track. It could be an echo. There must be lots of odd refractions of sound in a place like this.

But when eventually they arrived at the place where they were to find Bushman paintings, she forgot all her stupid fears in her delight at the scene around her. They had had to leave the mules and negotiate the last stretch on foot and the last few hundred yards had been a difficult scramble up steep hillside, but now they stood on a narrow plateau and behind them the rock formed a cave, very large but shallow, sheltered from the weather by an overhanging formation of the mountain.

It must have been an ideal home for the early Bushman people, for below could be seen the wide plain where great flocks of game must have once roamed.

'The Bushmen always chose their homes well,' said Stefan. 'I've never seen one yet that hasn't got a magnificent view.'

If he was sorry that he had had to bring Maggie along when otherwise he could have been alone with Carola in this beautiful lonely place he did not seem to show it, although Carola had insisted on having his help over the steep slopes and was now standing with her arm linked in his as if Maggie had no claim upon him in spite of the present situation.

He disengaged himself, a little embarrassed, Maggie supposed, that Carola should show her fondness for him so blatantly when he had been so disapproving of Maggie and Angus the night before, and turned towards the cave. Maggie gasped as her eyes became accustomed to the shadowy light. All over the inner walls were gloriously lifelike paintings of animals and people in glowing colours of brown, gold, black and white.

A huge eland stared with calm dignity at a female giraffe with her small long-legged offspring. Small figures with spears fled before a grey elephant, but others pursued a buck with bow and arrow. Stranger still, there were processions of weird creatures with human bodies but queer animal masks on their heads. They looked very similar to pictures of Egyptian friezes that Maggie had seen in museums. She felt a sense of awe as she looked at them. The surrounding landscape seemed so wild, and yet man had been here since the beginning of his existence. Stefan stooped to pick up a flint instrument from the floor of the cave.

'You have only to dig a little way in all these places to find all kinds of artefacts,' he said. 'Hammerheads, arrows, tools of all kinds. The Bushman lived a life like an early caveman. In the desert, they still do.'

Carola yawned. 'Don't let's get Stefan started on his hobbyhorse, Maggie,' she implored. 'He can go on for hours about the Bushman, how unmaterialistic he is, how close to nature, how it would be much better if we were a little more like him ... personally all the Bushmen I've met have been terribly unwashed and unattractive, I thought.'

Samgau was making his way quickly up the hillside. No, thought Maggie, one could not say these things of him with his heart-shaped face and his slow wise smile and his graceful way of moving. He was bringing a message that they were invited to take coffee and plum *kuchen* at the farm, and soon they had left the wild landscape and were sitting under the thorn trees enjoying the good things that Mr. Macpherson's wife provided. Boris had obtained all the pink quartz he required and it was to be carried back to the landrover by means of the pack mules.

How stupid she had been, thought Maggie, to feel so depressed up there on the mountainside. It was just because the scenery had been gloomy, that was all. Here at the farm nothing could be more homely as they were pressed to eat more *kuchen* and cream scones and their cups were refilled, while the farmer's young children and dogs romped around in the garden that had been lovingly cultivated in most adverse conditions.

The afternoon shadows had lengthened when they left to ride back along the gorge and the sun had slipped behind the mountain. When they reached this ravine again it had a depressing effect on Maggie's spirits as she rode through the narrow darkening defile.

This feeling was not improved when Stefan turned and in a half joking manner informed them that the ghost of a long-dead miner was supposed to haunt the place. 'He's supposed to have buried some gemstones and then to have lost track of them. Must have been a very forgetful bloke, for he doesn't appear to have found them yet.'

There was the harsh bark of a sentry baboon high up on the hillside and Maggie nearly fell from her mule. She thought she would be glad when they had reached the vehicle and were safely on their way home. Angus and Boris were behind her, but they seemed to have stopped to examine some rock and this left her alone and well behind Stefan and Carola. Her mule was lagging again and she tried to call out, but the path was so narrow and the others seemed far ahead. She supposed Angus and Boris would catch up with her soon. It was no use worrying, but she had never felt so alone, although this was stupid, for she knew the others were not far away.

Suddenly from the rocks above she heard a noise like a distant clap of thunder. Looking up, she was just in time to see a shower of rocks descending just above the place where she was riding. Far ahead she saw Stefan turn and shout at her, but she could not hear what he was saying, for stones were showering down around her in a terrifying noisy cascade.

She slid from the mule and crouched between its

body and the wall of rock, but still she felt sharp rocks graze her arms and head. She was so bewildered that she scarcely stopped to wonder how Stefan had got here so fast or how it was that he had her in his arms and was protecting her from the shower of rocks with the barrier of his own body. A huge rock fell and shattered beside them and then there was silence.

When Maggie opened her eyes, she was lying upon the ground with Stefan bending over her, and his face seemed to have a greenish pallor under the ruddy tan. But it's me that should be pale, she thought to herself drowsily. She had a sore bruised feeling all over her body and there were scratches upon her arms and legs. But fortunately the rocks seemed to have missed her head.

'Are you all right, Maggie? For God's sake, say something!'

Stefan's voice was rough and harsh and he was half shaking her. It was only when Boris rode up and remonstrated with him that he desisted from this rather drastic way of rousing her. Maggie sat up and Angus came with a clean handkerchief and a hat full of water that he had got from a nearby spring in the rocks. Between them they cleaned her up while Carola looked on rather impatiently as if she thought the rockfall had been specially engineered by Maggie herself so that they would all make a fuss of her.

'But what could have caused such a fall?' asked Stefan. 'The rocks round about here are usually pretty firm at this time of year. Certainly we haven't yet had rain to loosen them.'

'Could it have been the baboons?' asked Maggie.

'Hardly likely,' Stefan replied.

Perhaps not, but Maggie could have sworn that as

she looked up when the first thundering rumble came she had seen some kind of movement from the krantz directly above and a glimpse of a crouching black figure silhouetted against the narrow background of the rapidly darkening sky.

CHAPTER TEN

The large second-floor drawing-room had been cleared of most of its beautiful furniture and priceless rugs and the floor polished until it shone like golden glass, reflecting in its depths the Venetian crystal chandeliers with their intricate designs of blue and rose-coloured flowers encrusted with gilding.

It was the eve of the wedding, and tonight there was to be a dinner followed by dancing, for Sophia had insisted that Stefan's marriage should be celebrated in a proper fashion even though she had given her instructions from a sick-bed. At first Maggie had been worried about the effect of all this excitement upon Sophia's health, but it seemed she was thriving upon the fact that her plans for Stefan were coming to a climax.

She had long since disregarded the fact that it was an arranged marriage and treated it as if it were a true romance, for she could not believe that anyone could fail to be enchanted at the idea of marrying her beloved son. But Maggie felt as if she had been caught in some swiftly flowing stream and had reached a whirl-pool from which there was no escape. She lived from day to day not daring to think about the future. Suppose Sophia survived longer than the specialist had thought likely? On the one hand Maggie dearly hoped this would happen, but then what was to happen to her if she had to stay here ostensibly married to Stefan, pretending to be happy yet all the time living a lie?

How could she endure it if, when legally she herself was Stefan's wife, he still met Carola in Windhoek? Carola had vowed that they intended to continue their affair. And when Carola's divorce came through? It was best to live by the day and try not to worry.

On the surface her life seemed to be going according to fairytale traditions. For the ball Sophia had ordered for Maggie a beautiful white dress of filmy chiffon spangled with crystal beads so that it looked as if dew had fallen upon it. Silver shoes were adorned with crystal ornaments and her hair, which had grown a little longer since she came here, was to be tied back Grecian fashion with silver ribbon.

Sophia had sent Maggie's measurements to Johannesburg and the ball dress had arrived along with the flowers by special plane. Now the roses cascaded in pink waterfalls from white cornucopia while white cymbidium orchids mingled gracefully with green fern in old-fashioned silver vases. As the day wore on the small airfield looked like an important airport as it disgorged guests from numerous private planes. Special food and wine had been flown in too. There seemed no end to Sophia's ingenuity in her endeavour to do honour to Stefan and his bride.

Maggie's gift for organising, which had always made her popular with the orphanage staff, now surprisingly came to the fore in arranging this elaborate entertainment. She was here, there and everywhere, answering questions, soothing frayed nerves for caterers and waiters, deciding all kinds of small points.

Stefan came in search of her and found her at the top of a ladder demonstrating where they should put the garlands amongst the gilded mouldings of the drawing-room walls.

'The local press have arrived and want some photographs of the bride—informal, of course—then later they'll be taking more of the ball and the wedding.'

No one would have thought that this was anything but a marriage of love, Maggie reflected, as she and Stefan posed for the young reporter and photographer. Casually he put his arm around her as if he had forgotten his own ban, then at the photographer's insistence he tilted her face up towards his and they laughed into each other's eyes.

If only it were real, thought Maggie, with a dreadful pang of regret. If only it were not a sham on his part. But as soon as the newsmen had gone, his arm dropped to his side and his charming smile was replaced by a rather grim expression. 'Sorry about that, Maggie. There'll have to be more of it tomorrow. But you're a good little actress, aren't you?'

A better one than you know, thought Maggie. It was ironic that he should think she was acting when she looked pleased at his caresses when all the time it was the other way round and she had to dissemble the fact that his touch thrilled her, filling her with passionate tenderness.

Dinner that night was held in the panelled hall and the baroque Austrian table was set with an heirloom cloth of Brussels lace, elaborate heavy gold-plated cutlery, and a Sèvres dinner set that was over a hundred years old. For the first time Maggie had to act as hostess to this large gathering of friends and neighbours, for it had been decided that Sophia must conserve her strength until the actual wedding ceremony on the next day. She was determined to see them married and was willing to forgo her attendance at the ball if only she could accomplish this object.

If Matron could see her now! thought Maggie, as she took her seat at the end of the table, for it had been decided that she and Stefan, the bridal couple, should sit together. She had come a long way since she had had to preside at the orphanage high teas, and yet she was not overwhelmed by the grandeur of her surroundings. During the last few days of preparation, Sophia had vowed that Maggie became more and more like her mother, and perhaps that was it. Perhaps in spite of the orphanage upbringing the customs and manners of her forebears came easily to her.

But the kindness of the guests made it easy for her too. They were all enchanted by the fairytale sequel to her visit, only saddened by Sophia's ill-health, and Maggie, with her youth and bright sweet appearance, would make a charming bride. She appealed to them probably more because she was not perfect in appearance. It seemed to them rather piquant that Stefan, known for his penchant for female beauty, should have chosen a bride who was scarcely beautiful but on the other hand was full of natural charm.

Boris was a great help to Maggie in helping to entertain the guests and before dinner he had moved around amongst them quick to observe their needs. Even Angus, usually shy, seemed to make an effort to help the occasion to success. Only Alexis stayed in the background. Every now and again Maggie was conscious of his dark presence and felt him regarding her with saturnine frown.

She had hoped he would stay with his farming friends rather than stay here where he knew he was not welcome, but after that weekend he had spent away from the castle he had soon come back. He seemed to spend his time riding around the estate and was largely ignored by his relatives. Stefan could hardly bring himself to speak to him, but Alexis did not seem to mind all the coolness. He kept himself very self-contained, grinning occasionally as if he had some private jest.

Carola had come with a party of friends. She was looking very beautiful tonight, almost like a bride herself in gleaming parchment-coloured satin, a full-length dress very low cut to show the pearly curves of her exquisite figure. She sat well down the table and every now and again her laughter and that of her friends rang out, a little too loud for good manners.

When at a signal from Stefan Maggie took her cue that the women guests should leave the dinner table, she took them to a small sitting room where coffee was to be served. Only then, when they were away from Stefan's presence, did Carola approach her.

'How nice you look tonight, Maggie. I love your dress. Did Sophia choose it for you? Yes, I thought so. Just a trifle old-fashioned, of course, but most suitable, quite virginal in fact!'

She looked around at the gorgeous flower arrangements.

'Wonderful what money can do, isn't it, Maggie? Who would have thought when you first came that this was to be the sequel? I remember how Stefan laughed at your appearance that first day you arrived.'

Her barbed words had very little effect on Maggie, for she really did not have time to think of them. Doubtless they would come back to her later and worry her, but at the moment she had far too much to do attending to all the women guests, and from them she had so much praise and flattery that, although she knew it was not always quite sincere, nevertheless tonight her rather bruised ego blossomed like a crushed flower that has been restored to water. When a little later she was repairing her make-up she was surprised by the radiant face that looked back at her from the mirror. Come what may, she thought, she would enjoy this time with Stefan even if it led to heartbreak.

The Viennese orchestra had been playing soft lilting music from the gallery throughout the dinner, but now they were esconced on a raised dais in the flower-be-decked salon and were waiting for the signal from Stefan to begin the ball with an old romantic waltz.

As Maggie approached Stefan he came rapidly across the gleaming floor towards her and a kind of interested murmur rustled around the room as he took her in his arms and they started to dance. Stefan was smiling down at her as if she were the only girl in the world, and with her heart missing a beat, she felt annoyed for a moment that he could put up such a convincing pretence, but she remembered her resolve to enjoy this brief joy and she smiled up at him as if for her a dream had come true.

'Why, little Maggie, you look quite beautiful to-night,' Stefan murmured, his face against her hair.

'No one can hear you above the music, Stefan, so you don't need to pretend.'

'But I'm not pretending. You really do look very lovely.'

They had turned the central chandeliers off for dancing and in the subdued light of the side sconces his dark eyes were glittering with an expression she found hard to understand. Was he teasing her again? Oh, he was cruel to use her like this! Why had she consented to it? But there was no going back.

In spite of her resolve, her throat ached with unshed tears. How was she to get through the long evening? And next day too? She gave a tiny gulp, almost a sob, and blinked rapidly.

'Now what's wrong?' Stefan asked. He was far too intuitive, she thought ruefully. 'For God's sake, Maggie, can't a man say he finds you attractive without your bursting into tears?'

This was too much for her to stand.

'It's just that I hate your flattery that means exactly nothing,' she declared, and slipping away from him she went in search of somewhere dark and quiet where she could recover herself before going to her other partners. No one was on the small verandah yet, for everyone was too interested in the dancing. She leaned over the balustrade looking at the grey desert and the great silver globes of the stars hanging like lamps above this wild scene.

'What's the matter, Marguerite? Don't tell me you're suffering from pre-wedding night nerves?'

It was Alexis, the last person she wished to see, leaning against a pillar and smoking a cheroot. She could see its glow in the dark and the black glitter of his eyes. He walked silently towards her and she felt something of the shuddering repulsion that one feels in encountering a reptile. She moved to go towards the entrance into the salon, but he had seized her wrist in a grip of steel and on this dark balcony the lighted room and the gay dancers seemed a hundred miles away.

'No wonder you're feeling dubious about this business, Marguerite. Don't think I don't know that this is all a put-up plan. I should have thought a girl of character like you would have had more pride than to lend herself to such a scheme.'

167

'Let me go!' whispered Maggie. 'I'm not interested in anything you have to say.'

'Why did you lie to me? Why say you weren't interested in Stefan when all the time you were planning to spoil my chances?'

Maggie stared at him, her large brown eyes fixed upon him in terror as if hypnotised by a snake.

'And why did you act the innocent with me, tell me that? But let me tell you, Miss Marguerite, I don't forget easily when I've been insulted. I wasn't good enough for you, but Stefan, although you don't love him, is to be accorded the privileges of a husband, isn't that so?'

'No, strange as it may seem, it is not so!' Maggie was goaded into saying this, although immediately she wished she had held her tongue.

'You mean that you love him?'

Maggie was silent.

'Then the only other conclusion I can draw is that you think this is to be a marriage in name only? What a joke! How much has Stefan promised you to go through with this?'

Maggie hated this pawing over of her innermost emotions by a man she loathed. She tried to get free from him, but he gripped her more tightly still.

'You can't truly believe that a man of Stefan's temperament will be satisfied with a platonic marriage? After all, you're young and attractive, and Sophia will want grandchildren.'

'Alexis, I'm not prepared to discuss our coming marriage with you, so please let me go. Stefan will be wondering where I am.'

The steely grip was tight on her arm and with his other hand he drew her towards him.

'Isn't it a relative's privilege to kiss the bride?' he asked.

She was helpless in his arms that bound her to him like chains. It was like being kissed by some cold-blooded creature with no passion, only a dreadful desire for vengeance. Then gradually her numbed brain registered the fact that she was being pushed towards the low balustrade that was the only guard against the drop of a hundred feet below. Was this what he intended? She was frozen with terror, unable to struggle against the unrelenting grasp of his arms.

'Alexis? You also find my bride attractive?'

The hard grip relaxed so suddenly that Maggie nearly fell to the ground. She felt faint with relief. Stefan stood in the doorway surveying the scene with a satirical smile.

'This is no time to make a scene. But I'll discuss this with you later, my dear cousin. Come, Maggie. Our guests are waiting to toast us in the champagne cup.'

She was trembling all over, shaking with reaction.

'Stefan, I can't face them yet. You don't understand,' she said imploringly. But he shook aside her detaining hand. She realised that he was furiously angry.

'How dare you behave like a street girl with that monster?' he demanded. 'You, who pretend to be so cold! Is this the way you propose to behave in the future?'

'Stefan, let me explain.'

'Not now. There's no time. The show must go on.' His voice was infinitely sarcastic as he said this.

She did not know how she got through the next few hours. The champagne cup was brought in with much ceremony and applause. It was from an old recipe that Sophia's family had always used for special celebrations, made with strawberries, lemon and Marsala and white wine, left to mingle together for an hour before being mixed with the freshly opened champagne. The ceremony of serving it and of toasting the bridal couple was to the guests the crowning highlight of a perfect evening, but to Maggie, conscious of Stefan's icy disapproval and scarcely recovered from the shock of her encounter with Alexis, it was a dreadful ordeal.

Her face felt stiff with the smile she forced herself to give to all the wellwishers who pressed around them. Stefan laughed and joked with his guests, but never once spoke to her unless to give her some instruction. What was she to do? If she explained her fears about Alexis to Stefan it might lead to violence, and she must consider Sophia, for it would upset her considerably if the two men were involved in a fight.

But how could Stefan have thought she would willingly submit to his cousin's frightful embrace? That was bad enough, but had she been so unnerved that she had imagined the rest of it? Had she imagined that merciless grasp pushing her nearer and nearer to the edge of the balcony? She shuddered, scarcely conscious that Stefan had just put his arm around her in a casual way as he was responding to more good wishes. He withdrew it as the guest turned away giving her an enigmatic look. Of course he thought it was his touch that had made her respond in this way. How was he to know that it was the memory of Alexis?

At last the long evening was over and she was alone in her room where she found Serafina had pressed the dress she was to wear tomorrow and had left it hanging outside the wardrobe. She had had no opportunity to speak to Stefan alone, and really, she thought despairingly, there would have been little use in that. They seemed to be constantly at cross-purposes. How were they to live peacefully together when they were supposed to be husband and wife? And was it not a terrible sin that they were to take solemn vows without intending to keep them? She remembered what Alexis had said. Was it true that Stefan would not keep his word? The wedding dress gleamed against the dark cupboard like some fragile ghost in the shadowy room. She could scarcely believe that she was to wear it tomorrow ... no, today, for it was long past midnight.

CHAPTER ELEVEN

SOPHIA had consented to use an invalid chair to get from her room to the salon where the civil ceremony was to take place, and Maggie had come to help her to dress so that she could rest a little afterwards and get over the fatigue that this unaccustomed exertion entailed. She was to wear a very beautiful dress of grey cobwebby lace and a black mantilla and she had instructed Maggie to unlock the wall safe and bring out her finest diamond ornaments.

'Of course you yourself are to wear the tiara and the necklace of rose cabuchon diamonds,' she told Maggie.

'Oh no, please, Sophia. I couldn't wear anything so valuable. It must be worth a king's ransom,' Maggie replied.

'You must get used to wearing jewels,' Sophia said with a smile. 'One day they will all be yours.'

How complicated things became, reflected Maggie, when you started deceiving people. She was almost afraid to touch the elaborate necklace and small coronet because she felt she had not the slightest right to them. But Sophia insisted.

'You need not take them on honeymoon if you are so nervous for their safety, but every von Linsingen bride has worn these at her wedding. I am glad you have decided to fly to Swakopmund. I have always been very fond of that little house. I spent some of my happiest hours there. I feel it is a house for lovers.'

'Yes, it is a lovely place,' Maggie agreed.

She thought with bittersweet memories of the time she had spent there. How happy she had been when she walked with Stefan and gazed back from the jetty on to the little town, like something from an Austrian fairytale set amongst the wild sand-dunes of the Atlantic coast! She remembered how the waves seemed to murmur 'Stefan, Stefan!' How young she had been then, and yet it was only a few short weeks ago. It was there that she had first realised her love for him.

'I am sorry you will not be able to go to Europe just yet, but that will come later. When I have recovered, there will be plenty of opportunity for you to travel to Vienna and Paris and Rome with Stefan. You know he goes regularly there on business. It will be great fun for you, since he goes to all the famous fashion houses.'

She remembered how Stefan had teased her about her prejudices concerning Swakara or Persian lamb, how he had said that good farmers' wives wore them for advertisement. She still did not like the idea very much. He would have to go on considering her ignorant and naïve on that score.

The wedding was to take place in the evening just at sunset, and already it was three o'clock. With a trembling of the nerves Maggie realised that she must go and start preparing for the event. Sophia had protested that she should have stayed in her room and been spoiled with breakfast in bed and much cosseting as was the custom for a bride, but then, said Maggie practically, who would have seen to all the guests and all the arrangements?

As it was she had breakfasted with Sophia, but she had left to go to the kitchens before Stefan had appeared to visit his mother, so at least so far in that she had been conventional. She had not yet seen her bridegroom on her wedding day. She had had lunch in her own room so that at last she could have a little quiet.

Leaving Sophia, she thought she would have a stroll to get some fresh air before she started to change into her wedding garments. Where could she go? Most of the guests had retired to their rooms after lunch to rest before the festivities of the evening. She thought of the Garden of Love, such a cool beautiful place in which to stroll and sit beside the fountain with its beautiful exotic tiles and strange plants. There perhaps she would find some peace of mind before the ordeal she had to face.

But when she arrived there she found she was not alone. In the centre of the garden, dappled by sunlight that made patterns through the leaves of the sheltering trees, she saw Stefan and Carola sitting upon the bench by the fountain. She was too far away to hear what they were saying, but they both wore an expression of absorbed passion. Stefan got up as if to go, but Carola restrained him, holding his hands with both of hers. As Maggie gazed at the scene, unable to turn away, they seemed to come together in an ardent embrace, then just as suddenly Stefan broke away and strode out of her vision re-entering the castle by the other door.

So it was true. They did not intend Stefan's marriage to her should make any difference to them. She had known this in her heart but now faced with visual evidence she felt she could not go through with it. She must see him and tell him that he must keep his part of the bargain if she was to keep hers. Even if she was to be his wife in nothing but name, he must not be allowed to humiliate her by making love to Carola at every opportunity.

She was too late to overtake him before he ascended the stairs, but she saw his tall form at the end of the corridor leading to the tower room. Feeling that she must see him, she hastened to the small door leading to the other staircase. At her knock he flung the door open. His face was astonished. Had he expected Carola?

'Why, Maggie, what a surprise! I thought tradition had it that we were not to see each other until the ceremony.'

'What does it matter in our case?' said Maggie wearily. 'It's supposed to bring ill fortune, I've always heard, but we seem to be surrounded by that already.'

'What do you mean by that?'

Stefan's face was set. His brow drawn together in a grim frown. If this is what the prospect of marriage to me does to him, thought Maggie, remembering his gaiety on the first evening they had met, he would have been better far without me. She tried to find courage before his frowning gaze to protest at his behaviour.

'I saw you with Carola in the garden,' she stated baldly.

He looked a little taken aback, but quickly recovered his uncaring attitude.

'Oh, you did, did you? And what of it?'

'You appear to expect me to be circumspect, in fact already you've made ridiculous accusations against me, and yet there seem to be different rules for you, Stefan.'

Suddenly, unexpectedly, he put his two hands one on each side of her face.

'Look at me, Maggie. No, don't turn away,' for she had tried to avoid the penetrating stare of those hard grey eyes. 'I promise you that after today whatever the circumstances of our marriage, I will have nothing more to do with Carola or she with me. I was explaining that to her when you saw us.'

'But . . . Stefan, how can I go through with this? We must have been mad to think it possible!'

Stefan gave her a little shake.

'Pull yourself together, Maggie. This is all pre-wedding nerves. Quite natural, I understand. It always happens.'

She turned away. He was impossible! He spoke as if theirs were a normal marriage, but he knew very well that the whole thing was fraught with difficulties.

'You don't understand at all,' she protested. 'How did I ever get into this? I wish I'd never heard of the Castle of the Unicorn or of you either. I would be happy if I could go away today and never see you again!'

Stefan's face was stormy.

'You don't need to make it quite so clear how you feel about me, Maggie, but it's too late now. Look.'

Far below they could see the wedding guests strolling in the grounds of the castle. It had been a fine opportunity for all the neighbouring landowners to meet their friends and they were making the most of it.

It was true. It was impossible at this late stage to withdraw from this crazy plan. She must go to dress. She could not disappoint Sophia now. He moved forward to open the door for her.

'You may be sure I'll keep to my side of the bargain,' he said just before she descended the stairs. His eyes held the colour of steel in their grey depths. 'You understand what I mean?'

'I understand, Stefan.'

In a weary confusion of spirit, she made her way back

to her own room. She had refused Serafina's proffer-
red help, for she needed to be alone during this last
hour. The sun was still pouring down from the inter-
minably blue sky. It was like a bowl of blue, wearisome
in its monotony. Maggie found herself longing for grey
skies, damp soft mists, anything that would be a change
from this harsh hot land.

In the bathroom with the silver dolphins, Maggie
bathed, surrounded by the perfume of muguet. This
subtle fragrance, fresh yet sophisticated, had been the
favourite scent of Maggie's mother, Sophia had informed her, and to please the Baroness she had
accepted the soap, bath essence and cologne with this
unforgettable fragrance of the lily of the valley, the
scent beloved of French women.

How pale she looked in the long underskirt of cream
pure silk that was to be worn under the wedding dress!
As she applied a little make-up, her hands shook and
she was glad that at least in the first part of the ceremony a veil would cover her face, for she seemed
hardly to look like herself, with this transparent pallor
and the eyes that looked large and brown as those of a
hunted doe.

She was just about to put on the satin dress when
there was a knock at her door. Relieved to have company from her dark thoughts even if it was only Serafina, she put a short cream lace dressing jacket over the
sweeping folds of the cream underskirt and called
'Come in!'

Someone opened the door very quietly, but Maggie
thought nothing of this because Serafina was never one
to bang doors. But when no greeting followed in the
liquid African voice, she looked up from her seat at the
dressing-table mirror and was just in time to see Alexis

locking the door and slipping the key into his pocket.

Alexis! She tried to keep calm. Nothing must harm her now, for there was so little time left before the wedding was to take place. She tried to speak naturally although her heart was beating madly under the creamy folds of lace.

'Why have you come?' she asked.

Alexis laughed. It was not a pleasant sound and as he approached her a smell of raw spirits came towards her. His dark eyes were expressionless but glittering like those of a snake whose head is poised to strike.

'You didn't think, surely, little Marguerite, that I intended to stand aside mildly and let you and Stefan get away with the fortune that I was expecting? How foolish you must think me!'

'I've never thought you foolish or underestimated your ambition, Alexis,' said Maggie. Her voice was steady enough, although to keep it so was a great effort of will. 'But I intend to go through with this. Nothing can stop me now.'

'You think not? Ah, but, Marguerite, I'm afraid you're going to find you're sadly mistaken.'

While he was talking he had been edging her towards the fireplace wall, for she had no choice but to retreat as he came towards her. But now he seized her in a grip of iron, saying, 'It's not too late. If you change your mind about marrying Stefan, I'll take you back to Windhoek and you can catch the first plane out of the country. No one need even see you go.'

Although it was along these lines that Maggie had been thinking a little while ago, she shrank from the idea of escaping with Alexis as a companion.

'Don't be absurd, Alexis. What makes you think I

would be willing to leave? I couldn't let Sophia down now.'

'I notice you don't mention Stefan. It is Sophia you're thinking of, isn't it? What an admission for a bride! And you ask what makes me think you would be willing to leave. I think, my dear Marguerite, anyone would be willing to leave this situation rather than forfeit their life.'

The black reptilian eyes were menacing now, the thin arrogant face very close to her own as he slowly raised two thin ivory-coloured hands towards her throat.

'Which are you going to chose, little Marguerite, life without Stefan or death but still without him?'

'I'm not frightened of your threats,' Maggie asserted. She glanced towards the door. If only someone would come! How foolish she had been to make it so clear that she wanted to be alone before the wedding. There was no hope now even from Giselle, for she and Sacha had been closed in the tower room for the afternoon so that they would not insist on being with Maggie and Stefan at the ceremony.

As she looked away, she felt Alexis relax his grip upon her and she started towards the door, but she had only gone a few paces when she felt some kind of cloth placed over her face. There was a burning sensation and a sweetish smell. How odd, it must be because she felt giddy that the fireplace seemed to be opening inwards as if a door swung open! Before she lost consciousness, the thought came to her, 'Now Stefan will never know I love him.'

CHAPTER TWELVE

SHE woke to the terrifying revelation that she was a prisoner. At first she could only think with dazed relief that Alexis had gone and that she was alone. But where was she? She had never seen this room before nor had ever been told of its existence. It was a small stone cell, enclosed it seemed by the outer walls, for in the grey gloom there was a tiny slit of sunlight high above reflected from a small opening. The room was narrow and unfurnished except for the wooden monk's bench upon which she was lying.

Her head throbbed so that she found it difficult to concentrate. How long had she been unconscious? She had no means of telling the time, but if the sun was still shining it must still be afternoon. She could hear no sound. This place was like a tomb. She got up, swaying with a sickening vertigo and, after waiting a few minutes for this to subside, she slowly investigated the walls to find out where the room's entrance was.

She began her search methodically, not able to credit that her eyes would not adjust themselves to the dim light sufficiently for her to see the door of her cell. Then at last came the horrifying realisation that she could not find it. She could not find it because there was no door. She was in a small stone room that had no exit, walled in as effectively as a medieval nun who had transgressed her order's strict rules. The small slit of a room was at least thirty feet high and the aperture through which the sunlight penetrated was almost invisible, so far was it up the wall. There could be no help there.

How long did Alexis mean to keep her here? She supposed until after midnight, for if Stefan was not married by then Alexis would get the inheritance. For a moment she realised that she felt almost a kind of relief. The decision had been taken out of her hands. There was nothing more she could do, and she was not to make this strange marriage after all. But what about Sophia? The shock of her disappearance would be very bad for the Baroness. But they would try to find her. Stefan and Boris must know every inch of this castle. They must know a way into this room.

She began to wonder where she could be. Alexis could not have carried her very far without being seen. She racked her brains to remember those last moments before she had lost consciousness. Of course! The fireplace. It was no illusion that it had opened inwards. She must be in a secret room behind the huge open fireplace that was so much a feature of her tower room.

There must, however, be some record of it. In all his study of the castle's history, Boris must know about it. So she reassured her sinking spirits as the patch of sun on the wall slowly assumed a deeper hue of gold. Suddenly she became aware of something that she had half noticed before, but in her agitation she had not realised its significance to her present position. In the darkest part of the narrow room, where the tower met in a narrow curve, Alexis had placed her suitcases.

She went over to examine them and in the fading light she registered the fact that everything she possessed in the world was in this cell with her. Now why was that? Why had Alexis during the time when she was unconscious taken the trouble to pack all her suitcases and bring them in with her? Of course! He intended to make it look as if she had left the castle of her own accord. So no one would look for her, because no one would know she was a prisoner. They would come to her room and find that apparently she had departed with all her belongings like a servant who is too afraid to give notice so disappears without telling anyone.

But with whom then was she supposed to have gone? Alexis. Obviously once he had got rid of her he would go, because then it would make her supposed departure more feasible. She had reached this stage in her reasoning when she thought, he doesn't intend to come back for me. I really am like a nun walled up in a cell. He never intended me to escape. All along he intended me to die. He said so himself. He gave me the chance to go away with him of my own free will. But I refused, and then he promised me death.

At this her nerves broke and she hammered upon the wall where she thought the fireplace was and screamed for help, but for all the effect it had she might as well have been hundreds of feet under the ground.

At last she pulled herself together and tried to relax her trembling senses in order to assess her situation. After the first few awful moments she resolved that she must not give way to panic. Had she any means of attracting attention? she wondered. If she could find some matches amongst her luggage, she might light a fire with a little paper and rags from her clothing. Everything about her surroundings except the bench was made of stone, even the floor, so she could hardly set the place alight. But she did run the risk of suffocating herself, she thought after further consideration. There was no draught of air to bear the smoke directly out of the small slit in the wall. She could not incur this extra danger.

If she sat very still with her head near to the fireplace wall maybe she would hear if anyone entered her room. She crouched against the cold wall, straining her ears and imagining sounds that did not really exist, for it was too easy to do this, hampered as she was by the loud beating of her heart.

But probably whoever had been sent to fetch her, Serafina maybe, had come and gone, rushing down to the assembled guests to break the news that she had fled. She could not bear to think of Stefan's reaction. The fact that she had gone would confirm everything she had said during their last bitter scene. Would he be angry? She would rather that than that he should feel humiliated in front of all the guests. What would he think of her? He would think he had been wrong to trust her word when she had solemnly promised to marry him, or he would think that she had gone from bitterness after seeing himself and Carola in the Garden of Love.

The small patch of light had changed to deep golden red and now was slowly fading. Still Maggie sat on with her ears strained to catch the slightest sound beyond the wall. How could she endure to be left here in total darkness? How long did it take to die of starvation? A long time, she had once heard, for there was air here even if it was hot and lifeless. But she could not exist for long without water and there was no provision to drink here. In all the dungeons one reads about in castles overseas there would be a trickle of dampness down the wall that the parched prisoner would gladly sip, but here it was as dry as that desert that stretched beyond the walls to the cold grey shores of the Atlantic.

Suddenly as the light faded, she was startled by a small scratching sound. Oh heavens, there must be a rat in the cell! No, she could not endure the thought of the night with small animals pattering around her prison, revolting black-eyed furry creatures that with the onset of darkness would become progressively bolder. She screamed again and pounded her bare hands against the cruel tearing hardness of the relentless stone.

The scratching noise became louder and then in the midst of her extremity of terror she heard a sound that penetrated through her panic with the faintest gleam of hope. It was the yelp of a dog, a bell-like sound that could only come from the throat of Giselle. She started up, and as she did so the whole wall against which she had been leaning heaved itself heavily aside.

First there was Giselle, leaping around her, licking her face, with glad belling barks, thrusting her silky muzzle against Maggie until she could scarcely stand. And then she was safe again, for she was in Stefan's arms, grasped in a strong embrace that seemed the sweetest she had ever known. Her face was wet with tears and begrimed with dust, but he was kissing her as if he would never stop.

'Oh God, Maggie, I thought I'd lost you!'

She was holding his tawny head in her hands and looking up into his eyes that were grey as a storm and yet had lost their anger.

'How did you find me? How did you know?'

'When Serafina came to tell me you'd gone, I was mad with anger. But then I began to reconsider the facts. You would leave me, maybe, but I couldn't believe that you would go without leaving a message for Sophia. And I couldn't believe you would have taken the emeralds with you, or the diamond necklace and tiara. I'd felt uneasy for some time about Alexis and his intentions. I didn't say anything before because I had no wish to alarm you, but I mistrusted that episode in the ravine when you were knocked unconscious by a stone. It didn't seem like an accident to me.'

'I wish you'd said so,' said Maggie. 'I saw someone who must have been Alexis upon the high ground above. And, Stefan, he tried to push me over the tower—the time you thought he was making love to me.'

'What a fool I was! I should have known. But you'd been so cold towards me and I was mad with jealousy.'

Maggie's heart somersaulted. But if he was jealous, he must mean ...

'It was Giselle who found you. She wouldn't leave me alone after I'd released her when I began my search for you. Finally she led me here and scratched and barked at the fireplace. Then I saw a small fragment of lace caught in the crack. I rushed to Boris and he recollected that there was an old tradition about a secret room behind the fireplace in this room. Once we had his records it was easy to find the way to unlock the opening.'

'But Sophia?' asked Maggie. 'Is she dreadfully shocked?'

Stefan sighed. His expression was sad and yet somehow resigned.

'We haven't told her you're missing. Nor have we told any of the guests. They just think there's been some delay in the arrival of the plane that was to bring the marriage officer. We haven't let Sophia know that he's already arrived. We thought this small deception best for the time being.'

'So now,' said Maggie, 'she need never know. For I suppose the marriage can still take place and you will lose nothing.'

She was still held close in his embrace and as she said this he took her chin and tilted her face towards his, gazing searchingly into her brown eyes as if he would like to keep a picture of her in his heart for ever.

'You still have a very poor opinion of me, Maggie, and no wonder! But you must think me an absolute brute to believe that I would force you to go through with this marriage after an ordeal like this one.'

Maggie's heart dropped like a stone. How odd! This was what she had wanted to happen, and yet now...?

'What do you think we should do, then?'

'Do? Why, I suppose to tell the wedding guests that it's all off and then I'll fly you to Windhoek this very night and you can get the first plane out. No, Maggie, I wouldn't dream of keeping you to your promise now.'

'Do you mean this? But what about your inheritance? If we don't marry before midnight, you'll lose everything in the world that you value.'

'Do you really believe that, Maggie? Do you really believe that everything I value in life lies in the wealth of my father's possessions?' He gave a short sardonic laugh. 'But of course you would believe that. You've always thought ill of me. You don't even realise that since I've known you nothing else matters ... oh, what's the use of words? Get dressed and I'll take you to the plane. I'll tell Boris when we're ready to break the news to Maman and then the guests.'

He opened her suitcase and took out a dress and coat.

'Put these on. I can't leave you alone until you're safely out of the castle.'

186

He turned away and gazed unseeingly out of the window as she fumbled with the tangled knot of the lace jacket. She felt utterly confused. Must she really go away? But after her life here nothing anywhere else would mean anything. Was she to lose Stefan for ever? He seemed adamant that he would not marry her now. And yet there had been tenderness in his embrace and a promise of love.

The knot resisted all her efforts. She would have to ask Stefan for help. She went to stand near him as he gazed moodily out of the window and did not even notice her presence until she timidly touched his arm. Then he swung around and she was amazed by the savage misery in his eyes.

'I can't manage this, Stefan,' she said, indicating the stubborn knot. His hands fumbled over the tangled silk and all at once he gave a sudden groan and clasped her to him.

'Oh God, Maggie, don't you know, can't you realise that I adore you—but it's too late. Now you can never believe that I love you. Even if we were married to-night you would always have doubts that I'd married you to save my inheritance.'

She swayed before his passionate kiss, but as swiftly he let her go.

'For God's sake, Maggie, let's have done with this. Break that knot. What does it matter? You've already broken my life apart with your young charm that was never meant for me.'

'But I thought ... I thought ... Carola?'

'That was never love. When you saw us together this morning I was telling her it must end. She's leaving the country and may rejoin her husband. But what has that to do with us?'

There was a sound of laughter, a swift knock at the door and in burst several of the women wedding guests, laughing and talking.

'We have been sent to fetch you two. Whoever heard of the bridegroom being alone with the bride and making her late for the wedding? Aren't you coming now? Everyone is waiting.'

Stefan turned to Maggie with a gesture of despair.

'Tell them you're going,' his eyes implored.

But now she smiled and walked confidently towards him.

'Yes, we're coming,' she said. 'Stefan has been delaying us, but I'm almost ready now. If you could send Serafina to help me with my wedding gown I'll be down in a few moments. Tell the others I'm sorry we've been delayed. When you're in love you lose count of time.'

He made an involuntary movement towards her and she saw the longing and love in his eyes.

'Go down now, my dearest,' she said with utter confidence. 'Tell Sophia she won't have much longer to wait before she sees her son married to the daughter of her dearest friend. Tell her it's just what she and my mother dreamed about all those years ago, a marriage of true love.'

To our devoted Harlequin Readers:
Fill in handy coupon below and send off this page.

Harlequin Romances

TITLES STILL IN PRINT

51513   CHANGE OF DUTY, M. Norrell

51514   THE CASTLE OF THE SEVEN LILACS, V. Winspear

51515   O KISS ME, KATE, V. Thian

51516   THOSE ENDEARING YOUNG CHARMS, M. Malcolm

51517   CROWN OF FLOWERS, J. Dingwell

51518   THE LIGHT IN THE TOWER, J. S. MacLeod

51519   SUMMER COMES TO ALBAROSA, I. Danbury

51520   INTO A GOLDEN LAND, E. Hoy

51521   MY SISTERS AND ME, B. Perkins

51522   LOVE HATH AN ISLAND, A. Hampson

51523   HOUSE OF CLOUDS, I. Ferrari

51524   DEAR PROFESSOR, S. Seale

51525   THE UNKNOWN QUEST, K. Britt

51526   BRIDE IN WAITING, S. Barrie

51527   DILEMMA AT DULLOORA, A. Doyle

51528   THE MADE MARRIAGE, H. Reid

~~~~~~~~~~~~~~~~~~~~~~~~~~~~~~~~

Harlequin Books, Dept. Z

Simon & Schuster, Inc., 11 West 39th St.
New York, N.Y. 10018

☐ **Please send me information about Harlequin Romance Sub-scribers Club.**

Send me titles checked above. I enclose .50 per copy plus .10 per book for postage and handling.

Name ....

Address ....

City .... State .... Zip ....